RUN OF THE MILL

DAVE PATTEN

Published by:

G Street Chronicles
P.O. Box 1822
Jonesboro, GA 30237-1822

www.gstreetchronicles.com
fans@gstreetchronicles.com

This work is a work of fiction. The events and characters described herein are imaginary and are not intended to refer to specific places or living persons.

Cover design: Hot Book Covers,
www.hotbookcovers.com

ISBN13: 978-1-9384428-6-5
ISBN10: 1938442865
LCCN: 2013940809

Join us on our social networks

Like us on Facebook: G Street Chronicles
Follow us on Twitter: @GStreetChronicl
Follow us on Instagram: gstreetchronicles

To everyone who has done me wrong;
you're the reason I keep going.

Acknowledgements:

This book only exists because of my best friend Josh West, who is always there to push me forward in my moments of hesitation. Thank you for helping me through this book, and for editing this book. While much has changed from start to finish, one thing stays the same: there is never enough coffee or beer.

I'd like to thank my mom, Marilisa; my dad, Big Dave; my sister, Michele; and my brother, Sean, for always supporting me and my creative outlets, for never judging me, and for always, *always* loving me.

Thank you to my best friend David Ricks, for going to Hell and back with me and still sticking around. I owe you more than you know.

I'd also like to thank Shawna and everyone at G Street Chronicles for granting me the opportunity to live my dream and for publishing this book.

CHAPTER ONE

First Lieutenant James Miller stood in his Army camos with his arm outstretched, barely balancing on his two prosthetic legs, waiting for me to shake his hand. His eyes, along with those of everyone in the studio audience, including mine, were puffed red and welling with tears.

I shook it. He had the grip of a soldier, and the sunken, gray eyes of a man whose world was taken. A soldier who had lost everything but his pride. A soldier who sought me out for weeks, climbing through the jungle of assistants, production managers, and other idiots employed by my record label in order to finally get in touch with my manager, Jack, so that he could arrange this meeting live on national television; First Lieutenant James Miller wanted to personally thank me for writing the music that got him through the horrors of war.

I had never felt so worthless in my entire life. So ashamed of who I was; *what* I was. Everything to my name paled in comparison to what this man had accomplished. I wanted to curl up into a ball on the floor and shrink into nothing. The lights on the stage were so hot I could feel the sweat beading up on my forehead and neck. I prayed for a commercial break.

While First Lieutenant Miller raided hostile buildings in the scorching deserts of the Middle East watching his brothers in arms die in front of his eyes, I was prancing around on stage with my guitar with a halo of security guards ready to pounce on the next overly-aggressive girl trying to fight her way over the security gates. When Miller stepped on the IED that blew off his legs on the side of some dusty, abandoned desert road, I was singing to a sold-out crowd about my frustrations with failing to sleep with a girl I thought was hot. As First Lieutenant Miller laid in shock, instantly rendered immobile from the explosion, coloring the sands around him deep red with his blood, I sat in the VIP section of some pretentious nightclub in New York City or Miami or LA drinking free booze and banging cocaine.

I was proud to shake his hand. Proud to meet a true hero. His favorite song of mine was "On This Road, On My Own," he had told me before the show. It was a song I had written about never giving up.

I often wrote songs about the man I wish I were.

The show host, a petit woman in her forties named Anne, profoundly perky for 10:00 a.m., must have overheard our conversation backstage, because she decided to bring it up.

"Tell us, Tyler, what inspired you to write your hit single 'On This Road, On My Own?'" she asked. "I know it's Lieutenant Miller's favorite song of yours!"

At a certain point during a press tour, answering questions like these becomes second nature. The whole charade becomes routine; you've been doing it for so long that you no longer have to bother thinking about what to say. You smile, nod, and mindlessly talk. Mechanics. But the goddamn lights were so hot I couldn't concentrate; and I was hungover as all hell from the night before, and Anne was so fucking caffeined up that I wanted to just sock her in the mouth so we could all enjoy a few seconds of silence.

"It's an old song. I wrote it when I was maybe fourteen." I said. "It's about fighting for what you believe in, and never giving up. It's everything I wish I could've done, but didn't have the guts to do. I regret a lot of my life."

Her face went white. Talk show hosts—especially morning talk show hosts—*hate* when their guests give negative responses. They always want everything to be so perfectly upbeat and fun. The PR people will teach you that, too, in what they call "publicity training." Mine was a four-day crash course in Beverly Hills on interviewing and maintaining the proper elegance and poise a celebrity who is constantly in front of cameras needs to sustain. Their number one rule: always agree. *Say yes*. Don't be difficult. Talk shows, red carpet interviews, industry gala events—they're all the same. They want good news. Don't deliver the bad.

But Anne was really pissing me off this morning.

"Well, you have quite a resume to your name, I don't think the Tyler Clark we've come to know and love has been any bit of a failure," she said with a big smile into the camera.

"I'm not talking about failures, I'm talking about regrets." I said. "Do you know what I had to do to get here?" Lord knows, I did some horrible things. "Do you realize how many immoral, non-ethical, and illegal things I had to do, just to sit in this chair?"

She giggled and waved her arm dismissively. "Certainly all good things take time… I'm sure you had quite the mountain to climb!" Her eyes shot furtively to the Program Director standing off camera. He gave her a bored shrug. She glanced at Lieutenant Miller, looking to him for help, but his face was stone.

"I'm here because of First Lieutenant Miller," I said. "If anyone deserves the spoils, the money, *the women…*" The audience laughed. "It's men like him. Not me."

"We've all done things we regret." Lieutenant Miller interjected. I shifted my weight in my seat. I wasn't expecting him to jump in. I don't think anyone was. Anne let out a louder sigh of relief than she probably intended to.

"I'm sure you've done some bad things, Tyler. We all have." Lieutenant Miller looked out at the audience as if trying to decide whether or not to go further. "I've killed a lot of men."

A sea of whispers swept up from the audience.

"I've killed innocent people…people who did nothing wrong—women, children—people who were caught in the wrong place at the wrong time." He swallowed hard. "*That's the cost of war!'* My Generals would tell me." He slapped his prosthetics with his hands. "We all pay back our debts, in one way or another. These guys paid mine."

The room went quiet. "It sounds like guilt and loneliness are your currency," he said. The cameras turned and all eyes were on me, waiting for my reaction. Hoping I might snap.

You can't let weakness show. You can never let inner turmoil sneak through the cracks of your superficial celebrity presentation. That would only ruin you. The falsehood would be gone, the curtains drawn. I had to push past it, keep cool, maintain the image.

Those goddamn lights were so hot.

"Who am I to judge?" he continued. "No one. That right is reserved for God, and I know that." He turned from the audience and locked eyes with me. "But please don't ever forget, the music you write and give to the world has done amazing things for a lot of people. It *literally* saved my life. You've helped a lot more people than you give yourself credit for, Mr. Clark." The audience erupted in applause. "It seems to me that you may have gotten everything you've ever wanted—the fame, money, girls—but you still haven't found what you need."

I could feel my heart break in two the moment those words passed from his lips. He was right. I was alone, and I was empty.

"When we come back, we've got a treat for you guys!" Anne cut in, shouting over the audience, completely ignoring the conversation at hand. "Tyler Clark is going to perform a song for us off of his new album! Stay tuned, we'll be right back!"

WWW.GSTREETCHRONICLES.COM

CHAPTER TWO

I ignored my phone buzzing in my back pocket for the millionth time. It was probably my publicist, freaking out about the interview with Lieutenant Miller. I guess it did kinda get away from me, but it's a lot of damn work being all smiles all the time, and I get exhausted pretending life is but a dream.

I was standing side-stage in the thick concrete halls of the Electric Factory on 7th Street downtown. I couldn't stop thinking about Lieutenant Miller, and how different our lives were, or the fact that he had seen more before his twenty-second birthday than I would in the rest of my life. I was jealous. I wanted to trade lives. I wanted to know that feeling of camaraderie, friendship, pride, and loyalty that comes with war. I wanted to have someone's back, a brother in arms that I would die for. I wanted someone in my life that I could trust would do the same for me.

I know if I stopped making money right now, everyone around me would disappear.

Everything I've accomplished in my career I've done by exploiting my experiences. Exploiting my life. I'm an "artist," so I guess that's how it goes, but the internal struggles and torture you go through as an "artist" are a necessity I am not a fan of. The guilt is immense and unruly, and the past never seems to leave. I thought I'd figured out how to bury mine, but no method truly works. Sobriety breeds insanity. Women are a Band-Aid. Drinking and drugs just end with an empty bank account and more crying over spilt milk. I only have one escape, and that is the music I write, which I can only write well when I write about my past experiences, past loves, and past losses. It's a vicious cycle.

When I was sixteen years old my world changed. I was forced to become an adult too soon, and as a result, I've never fully grown up. I took refuge in immaturity. It was more comfortable to keep acting like a kid than to face the realities of adulthood. My best friend Kyle and I had things figured out better back then than I do now, that's for sure.

Now at twenty-six, I was "living the dream" as defined by most. On paper, I was a successful musician signed to a major record label; I toured the world, released albums, shot music videos, got paid to party at clubs, got paid to wear brand-name boots or jeans or jackets or ties when I hit the red carpet, got paid to talk, walk, eat, and sleep; I went to the biggest parties and hung out with the most famous celebrities. I made around two million dollars a year *after* taxes. I had a house in the Hollywood Hills, and one in my hometown of Philadelphia. I only lived in those houses about four weeks out of the year, as I was on the road constantly touring; but you wouldn't hear me complain. Not about music. Talk show hosts and pretentious "Hollywood" jerkoffs, yeah. But never music. I loved waking up in my dingy 1970's era tour bus, in a different part of the country every other day, changing my guitar strings over a hot cup of coffee in the chilled air and early morning sunlight, and taking V for walks through new cities and country sides. Spending 9/10ths of the year playing music was exactly how I wanted to live my life. I just hated the way fame works.

My manager, Jack, was my closest friend, second to my dog, V (short for Voldemort), who was just about the only living, breathing, creature on earth I could truly trust. Take the shirt off my back and you'll see all the knife wounds.

"You ready?" Jack asked, sneaking up behind me.

"What do you mean, *am I ready*? Of course I'm ready. When am I ever not ready?" I still get nervous before my shows and I hate it when Jack busts my balls about it.

"Jesus, Ty. You've been actin' like a fuckin' muppet since the talk show this morning. Was that you in the bathroom just now? Crying to yourself, havin' a wank?"

Did I mention he was Irish?

"I hate you so much sometimes."

"*Ahh* come off it. You're still only twenty-six," he said.

I've always said that if I hadn't "made it" in music by my twenty-seventh birthday, I would quit the industry and join the Marines. That's probably why I was so shaken up from meeting Lieutenant Miller earlier today. I've always loved the military; probably a direct result of growing up with my Granddad, an Air Force Vet, and from playing video games like *SOCOM* and *Call of Duty* for so many hours of my teenage years. Making the cut to join the Marines would be an especially proud moment for me.

"It's the last show of the tour," he said.

"I know, Jack, but thank you again for the reminder."

"Big crowd."

"Yeah."

"Sold out."

"I see that."

"Don't want to fuck it up! In your hometown…last show of the year…"

"How about if I fuck up, you don't get paid?"

That soured him.

"Not in the joking mood, huh? Alright, fair enough."

"Oh, were you joking? Because I wasn't."

"I'd call you a cunt, but you lack the depth and warmth," he said, snickering to himself.

The fact that he was actually pretty clever made his tirades even more annoying. Jack was like a mean older brother to me; he was bigger, better looking, and constantly bakin' my scrod. He was great at managing my tours, but always pursued a separate agenda once the work was done. I didn't see him much outside of rehearsals and shows. Not to mention, the minute he introduces himself, all the girls fall in love with him. Jack West and his stupid accent. It's infuriating sometimes, seeing how easy it is for him. And he's not one to let opportunity pass him by.

"I *do* need to concentrate a bit to do this. I know you don't have a clue what it's like to perform or play an instrument, but it does take some effort." I said.

"Alright…alright…" he said, walking off. Jack also taught me damn near everything I know. He's the reason I have a career.

The lights dimmed and the audience went wild; the show had begun. I got the "go, asshole" signal from Jack, plugged in my in-ear monitors, and double-checked my guitar tuning. I tour with an eight-piece band: drums, guitar, piano, bass, and three horns. They had already started to play my intro song and were waiting for me to join them on stage.

I bowed my head and transformed. Slipped into the Tyler Clark skin my city of Philadelphia had grown to love and expected to see. I can't speak for all performers, but when I jump on that stage, I go to a different place. I know how hippy and artsy that sounds, but it's the truth. Once the intro music starts, my mind fizzles out. At first it's like a drunken dizziness, where everything around me starts to blur, and then everything disappears. I slip into auto-pilot mode. I honestly have little recollection of what happens between when the intro song starts and when I shout my final words into the microphone to end the show. I'm just happy I make it through every time.

This show in particular was incredible. There were fourteen thousand people in attendance, and from up on stage it seemed as though every person in the building were a diehard fan. Epic applause at the beginning and end of each song, crowd surfing, sing along chants. Stopping the music in the middle of the song to hear thousands of fans screaming your words back to you is an unbelievable experience. It's always great to be back in your hometown.

I was fortunate enough to make a lot of good decisions in the past few years, and as a result, my music exploded. My fan base quadrupled. This was the first tour I'd done in a few months since our last route overseas, and the first Philly show I'd played in over a year. It was a huge finale for the tour.

We *crushed* it. The crew was on cloud nine after the show. We piled into our blacked out Cadillac truck and hit a club on Walnut Street called *Coche* which, in my previous experiences having lived most of my life in Philly as a very unimportant person, was always a bit too bombastic for me. I usually avoided it. Their watered-down drinks were fifteen bucks a pop, and it cost forty dollars just to get in.

This time was different though. I was being *paid* to show up and drink; a few different sponsors were covering the bill. It's difficult not to have a good time when you're labeled *VVIP*. All bottles, food, and drinks were taken care of, and I was making fifteen thousand bucks just to be there.

I'm not sure there's anything more valuable in America than fame.

A few hours later, I was drunk. The good kind of drunk, before things get sloppy. I went to talk to this cute blonde chick to invite her back to the VIP section the club had roped off for me. I couldn't stay at our table any longer. Jack had already left with a group of four girls to explore God knows what sexual odyssey, leaving me stranded with Richard, our extraordinarily creepy bassist. He had a jet-black *Just for Men* goatee, was nearly bald at 29, and wore this horrible, diarrhea-brown leather jacket with those cowboy tassels on the shoulders. He looked like a pedophile. I couldn't sit there alone with him at the table, people might start to assume things. The paparazzi love nothing more than the opportunity to stir up and sell off drama. I told Richard I had to use the restroom, and that I'd be back in a few minutes.

The cute blonde girl had been eyeing me up for the last half an hour, so I figured I had a decent shot; maybe we'd dance a little, have a few more drinks, and exchange numbers. She was even better looking up close.

Then she opened her mouth. She sounded like one of those rag dolls, the ones where you pull the cord on their back and they shout *'I love you!'* in that creepy horror movie voice. She wouldn't stop screaming over the music, right into my ear. I mean right up in there. It felt like she was jackhammering my brain. I jumped back a little and spilled my drink on her high heels, which amplified her shrieking to a near-impossible level. She and her girlfriend ran off into the bathroom, giving me dirty looks and yelling more words that I couldn't hear, because I was checking my inner ear for blood.

CHAPTER THREE

There was a sweet stickiness to the air in the back alley. I was subtly swaying in the middle of my circle of bodyguards, waiting for the Caddy truck to arrive and take me back to the Westin on 17th Street.

I was thinking about the Electric Factory show, and a couple of the chords I had missed on my guitar during two of the songs towards the middle of the set. Those tiny mistakes always pissed me off. I'd never put on a flawless show. It bothered me.

Then I saw her. She had on a tight pair of dark jeans with a leather jacket and a loose white blouse. She introduced herself as Rachel Helms from the *Philadelphia Inquirer*. She had long, brown hair that stopped right below her neck where a small necklace dangled. She carried a notepad in her right hand, and a pen in her left. Upon approaching my wall of security guards, her expression changed from determined to slightly regretful. She started clicking her pen nervously. I don't blame her, I'd be a tad apprehensive too, walking up to the guarded celebrity and his three towering body guards with their concealed handguns and military grade buck-knives at 2:00 a.m. in a back alley of

Center City Philadelphia, the murder capital per capita of the United States. The damn city couldn't even make it to January 31st of the new year without more reported homicides than days. I spent a lot of time in my early twenties running from gunfights in North Philly. I can attest that those numbers are accurate.

I gave Pudge, my head of security, the signal to relax a bit as she approached. He and the guys backed down. I couldn't help but chuckle as I watched Ricks (he was my favorite in the crew; nicest guy in the world) slowly withdraw his hand from his pistol and clip it back into its holster. He was always on edge. As a former Marine with six tours in the Middle East under his belt, he'd been through hell and back.

The cloud of security dissipated and I could finally see Rachel in the yellow tint of the street lamp. She was beautiful.

"I know it's late and this is really *really* bad timing," she said. "I'm Rachel."

"Tyler."

"Would you be able to give me just five minutes for an interview for *The Inquirer*? I tried to get to you after your show at the Electric Factory earlier, but security wouldn't let me through." She eyeballed Ricks, who was staring straight ahead like a British Royal Guard at Buckingham Palace. "My deadline is…uh…in a couple hours."

Her smile and obvious desperation were so cute, and I was feeling good, and the Caddy truck couldn't have pulled up at a more perfect time, so I obliged.

"Do you like coffee?" I asked.

"Of course."

"The restaurant in my hotel has great coffee." It doesn't. "Let's talk there."

I opened the door to the Escalade all chivalrously, and signaled for her to climb aboard.

"Thanks," she said as she passed in front of me. I could tell from her smile and the light brush of her hand against my leg that this was going to be a great interview.

WWW.GSTREETCHRONICLES.COM

CHAPTER FOUR

We didn't drink much coffee, and the interview didn't last more than two minutes before Rachel was on top of me. Grinding, ripping off my belt as I pulled her shirt over her head. The penthouse suite was massive. It was the only room on the entire floor; when you opened the heavy wooden double doors, you were staring at a wall of glass overlooking the entire city; three hundred and sixty degrees. On the East side, the Delaware River sparkled with the lights of the Ben Franklin Bridge, still busy with traffic late into the night. It was close to 3:00 a.m. now.

I opened the window and let the air rush in, three thousand feet up. It was shockingly refreshing, like stepping into a cold shower. I finally shook out the stress and worry that'd been crawling around in my head since this morning. Lieutenant Miller said it himself; *I shouldn't be so hard on myself all the time.* I had just performed for an audience of people so large that only a handful of other humans in the *history of the world* could say they've done the same. I came from nothing, and created a dynasty. I had the wealth and the influence a lot of power-hungry men would kill for. It wouldn't *kill me* to enjoy some of the perks. Maybe crack a smile once in a while.

Rachel slipped her arms around my chest, kissing my neck as she hugged me. I found solace in her touch, even if it was only for the moment. The fleeting pleasure of a one-night stand; for the next few hours, I was hers and she was mine.

I felt her hand slip over my shoulder and down onto my chest as she kissed my neck. She dropped to her knees in front of me. I stopped thinking and just lived, letting the cool air paint my face. I tilted my head back and let out a long, slow, breath.

I woke up the next morning to the sound of shower pipes squeaking off and a knock at the door. Rachel stepped out in just a towel and answered cheerfully; breakfast was served. She'd ordered up a bottle of Bollinger with our meal. What a great woman. I needed another drink to kill the rager of a headache I felt sneaking up.

"Good morning," she said softly, crawling up to me in bed. Her towel slipped down her breast. She kissed me. "I was thinking we could finish our interview over breakfast."

"You mean the interview is a real thing?"

"Yes, it's real," she said, coyly. I made my way over to the coffee table as she pulled out her notepad and a small tape recorder. I poured two cups of coffee and stuffed a croissant in my mouth.

"How many questions do you have?" I wasn't trying to be a dick; I'm just not too hot on interviews. Especially Saturday morning interviews, when we could be doing other things…

"Not that many," she said. At least it wouldn't take long.

"What happened to that deadline you were talking about last night? Haven't you missed it?"

"No… not yet."

She took a nibble from one of the croissants, and then daintily placed in on a napkin. She ripped open a sugar packet and three creamers, dumping them all into her mug. It killed me watching her destroy a perfectly good cup of coffee like that. God, I wanted to kiss her.

"A little coffee with your cream there?" She was busy looking at her notebooks. I don't think she heard me. "When is it?"

"When is what?"

"The deadline."

"Oh…It's soon. So we'd better get a move on," she said, shuffling around.

Something about the way she was acting seemed fishy to me. "You don't have a deadline, do you?" I caught her forcing back a grin as soon as I asked. She made this whole thing up. "Do you even work for the paper?" I asked.

She laughed. "Yes! I swear."

I waited silently for more, sipping my coffee, leaning back in my chair.

"Ok…so…I *may* have made up the deadline…but I wanted to get to you last night," she said.

Good enough for me.

"And I *do* have to interview you. They're giving me a front page spread in next Sunday's music section."

"That's great. Congratulations," I said, housing another croissant.

She bowed her head and continued reviewing her questions, crossing her legs and scrunching her brow, running her finger under each line of ink she had scribbled down. Every now and then she would exhale, deep and slow, brushing her hair back behind her ears.

"Excuse me a minute," she said, briskly walking back into the bathroom.

I leaned back, gazing out at the skyline surrounding me. The view was even more pleasant during the day. We were so high up that the traffic below us was silenced, replaced by the occasional bird chirp, or the low humming of a passing airplane. For the most part it was just the breeze. A light, warm, happy breeze.

"Ok," she said, breaking the silence. I heard her clicking her pen again. She seemed overly nervous for a reporter, even a rookie one. Especially after last night. Maybe she was still embarrassed about her faux-deadline.

I grabbed the bottle of Bollinger. The little towel for the champagne cork was sitting at the far end of the table and I didn't feel like moving or asking her to pass it, so I popped the cork without it. It shot across the room, knocking over both of the wine glasses left out on the counter from the night before. Rachel let out a shout in surprise. I couldn't help but smile.

"Drink?" I asked.

She politely declined, so I kicked my feet up and sat back, gaily sipping my thin flute of bubbly. I couldn't help but smirk, thinking about pulling that skimpy hotel towel right off of her and carrying her back to bed.

But she wanted to work now, so I did my best to behave. I admired her focus.

Then my mind wandered off and thought about how much the hotel was going to bill me for those two shattered wine glasses, which completely killed my vibe. I should have just asked her to pass the towel.

She was clicking her pen a million times a minute now. It was incessant.

"Do I make you nervous?" I asked, staring at the pen.

"Yeah…I mean no, I'm not nervous. You don't make me nervous at all. I'm ready, sorry," she said. She clicked on the tape recorder. "I want to talk about your early days as a musician."

"Not much to talk about," I said. Reporters always brought this up. My past would never stay buried, no matter how hard I tried.

"Nothing?"

"I sucked at guitar, practiced my guitar, got a little bit better. It's a simple history. The real story started when I turned twenty."

"Twenty?" she said.

"Yep, when I moved to LA to pursue my dream. This dream," I said, pouring another glass.

There was a long pause. She wouldn't look me in the eye, and seemed terrified of what she was about to ask. This had actually turned into the most intriguing interview I'd had in months; years, even. I felt compelled to help her out.

"A year later I landed my record deal at Atlantic, which changed my life. I wouldn't be here if it weren't for them. Did you know Led Zeppelin was signed to Atlantic Records? I recorded my first major album in the same studio Jimmy Page cut *Led Zeppelin II*." I said.

Click. Click.

"You have a unique way of conducting your interviews." I smirked, trying to come across like I was teasing her, or flirting. It didn't work.

Click click click click click.

"Let's dig a little deeper, then," she said.

"I already told you, there's nothing--"

"Let's talk about Kyle Hall."

The pen stopped clicking.

"What?" I blurted it out. I stopped moving. How this chick knew who Kyle Hall was I didn't know, I didn't want to know, and I didn't care. I don't talk about Kyle Hall. I don't even like to *think* about Kyle Hall. I wasn't going to start now. "Kyle was an old friend of mine from a long time ago. That time has passed; I haven't heard from him in ten years."

"What exactly happened that caused the two of you to lose

touch?"

"Next question please, Rachel," I said.

I could tell she wasn't going to give up without a fight. Young reporters are always out to prove themselves, trying to venture into the uncharted Far East of journalism to make a name for themselves by asking questions that no one else has ever asked. What they don't realize is that they've got their equation backwards; it's not that no other reporter has ever had the balls to ask their question. Believe me, they have. Most new reporters have egos, and their gigantic egos blind them from the reality that *every* reporter has already asked their dumbass question. They've just never seen it published because none have ever been given an answer.

"I'd like to know… our *readers* would like to know what happened between you, Kyle Hall, and Jules Levin in the summer of 2002."

Wait. *Jules Levin?*

My stomach pitted up; I hadn't heard that name in years. A piece of me was gone, forever, because of Jules Levin. Now I know why Rachel was so nervous. She had dug extremely deep… and she knew exactly what she was getting into.

Kyle Hall and Jules Levin were a part of a past that I had tried forever to keep hidden, and had done so successfully as far as my professional music career was concerned. My own personal struggles with it weren't relevant when it came to talk shows, interviews, albums, and tours. If you wanted to make it as an artist in America you had to be able to separate your person from the product. I had to, at least. There were two Tyler Clarks in my life; one who could handle it, and one who couldn't. Jules Levin was one of those people *neither* Clark could handle.

"Is there a reason your readers want to know about that year in particular? I write lots of songs about lots of different times in my life." I said.

She reached over and turned the tape recorder off.

"Fuck the readers. *I* want to know what happened." Her voice was at first stern, and then turned soft, almost scared. Her tone bit with vengeance. I didn't know what the fuck was going on in this conversation. In the last four minutes I watched her go from pleasant to nervous to passive-aggressive and back. I thought *I* was the nutty one. What happened to the morning sex I was just daydreaming about? I wanted to go back to that.

"Listen, Rachel, I don't think you understand how this works."

"I do. And I'm going to give you one more chance to tell me."

"Tell you what?" I could feel my voice heightening.

"Tell me what happened to Kyle Hall."

"How the hell do you even know who he is?"

"That's not important."

"It kind of is."

"I also want to know how you got here. How you became so successful *overnight* after what you did."

"I can assure you, none of this happened overnight."

"Are you going to tell me?" she asked. I stood, staring. Incredulous. "Do you even remember what happened?"

"I remember a lot of things."

"So tell me."

"I'm done. This interview is over." I said. I have a short temper for bullshit like this.

I stood up and walked over to the couches. Five minutes ago I was ready to bang this chick to oblivion. Now I couldn't help but fantasize about tossing her out the window. Out of the corner of my eye I saw her stand up and take a few steps towards me.

I conjured up a follow-up retort. I needed something sharp enough to make her pack up her things and leave, right now.

Or I could just have her escorted out…*where was Ricks when I needed him!?*

Rachel's towel dropped to the floor. I turned. Wow. That was quick. Really quick. I guess I could be pretty persuasive when I wanted to be. Maybe she'd gotten the hint and was finally coming around? Unlikely, but I'm a dreamer.

"Holy shit." I let out a gasp.

Jesus, was I wrong. She had no intention of messing around. Her perfectly tanned skin was now covered in deep reddish-purple bruises and welts, from her ankles to her neck. The towel had hidden them before. It looked like someone had taken a belt to her. *My* belt; I could see the outline of the buckle face imprinted on her abdomen.

"Rache…" My throat felt like it was swelling up. I was going to be sick. The mutilations were horrific.

"You did this to me, Tyler" she said.

"What?"

"You did this to me."

"I didn't fucking do any of that to you."

"You raped me, Tyler," she said.

"What?" It was like my body seized up. All I could do was stare, furious, and terrified.. I couldn't look away.

She bent down and picked up her tape recorder, holding it to her ear, rewinding it, and then pressing the *PLAY* button.

"Stop, stop, stop! Tyler!" her voice cut through the silence of the suite like a sharp knife. She had recorded the sex from last night. She fucking recorded our sex and was trying to use it in some sort of extortion scheme.

"*Don't! Ugh! Oh… oh, oh, oh God Tyler! Tyler Clark!*"

Then my voice cut in. "*Shut up. Shut the fuck up! What's my name? What's my name, bitch?*"

I'll admit, I sometimes get a little carried away in the bedroom.

Last night was wild, and Rachel was adventurous. It was fun to get rough, to pull her hair, have her slap my face and claw me, calling each other names. She was the one who encouraged most of it. Conniving bitch.

"Tyler! Tyler Clark! Please, please, stop!"

This self-mutilating psychopath was trying to extort me for my money. And listening to the tape back, it did kind of sound like she was really trying to get me to stop…not good. Not good at all. In court, the jury would find me guilty after hearing three seconds of that tape, regardless of my defense. She had me cornered. These fake-rape cases involving celebrities always end up in court; the girl and her scumbag lawyer want as much attention drawn to their case as possible so that the defendant, aka *me*, will be pressured to pay out a boatload of cash in settlement to keep things quiet and to save my reputation.

She clicked *STOP*. Her eyes bore into me. I could feel my fists clench and my posture change, naturally shifting defensively.

"You want money." I said. They all want money.

"You raped me, Tyler."

"Cut the shit, alright? Just tell me what you want, I'll pay it now and you can leave. We don't need to go through the whole court circus. And, by the way, the tape would have sufficed. You didn't need to go and beat yourself up like that. You're a goddamn mess. We need to get you to a hospital to have that checked out. I'm not having your blood on my hands, too."

"I don't want money" she said. I scoffed. Yeah, right. "I want the truth. The truth about what happened with you and Kyle."

"Jesus Christ what is it with you and that kid? It's pretty obvious you know him somehow, why don't you just ask *him* what the fuck happened?"

"I need to hear it from you," she said.

I was really starting to get heated. This was some bullshit.

"You forced me into your hotel room and tore off my clothes. You threw me onto the bed and--"

"How much do you want for the tape, alright? I'll cut you a check right fucking now--"

"I don't want your money! I WANT THE TRUTH!"

There was a cold emptiness and loss in her eyes; both ferociously angry, and tremendously sad. It was starting to terrify me.

I lunged for the tape recorder.

"Go ahead. I already made digital copies," she said. "If you want, I can have my lawyer send you one."

Fuck.

"…Please tell me you didn't send it out already." I said.

"Not yet."

This girl wasn't one of the dumb ones. She'd clearly thought this through, and wasn't going to give in until she got what she came for. I pressed my hand against my forehead and squeezed, hoping to relieve some of the pressure throbbing against my skull. I tried desperately to think of a way out of this. She had me, checkmate.

I took off my robe and extended it to her. "Would you please put this on?"

She slipped the robe over her tortured body and sat down on the couch.

"If I tell you, can we come to an understanding about…all of this?" I asked, motioning to the tape recorder and her legal pads. She nodded her head. "Where do you want me to start?"

I had no other choice.

"You know where," she said.

"Are you sure we can't go to the hospital first?"

The look on her face made it pretty clear she had no intention of going anywhere.

CHAPTER FIVE

1996

I grew up an only child in a tiny section of West Philly, where the houses actually had front lawns and backyards, and the trees grew healthy and tall. It was the 90's; times were good. I had a green Mongoose BMX bike and a PlayStation; life was good.

After school I traded Magic and Pokémon cards, but I wasn't super-hardcore about it. I didn't spend all my allowance every week on new packs, or hang out at game stores on Friday and Saturday nights dueling, mostly because I couldn't find a ride to the mall, and because the kids who played Magic were pretty big assholes. I was good at sports, but I didn't like them enough to go all O.D. and join the club travel teams; so I didn't hang out much with the sports kids either. The one person I did hang out with was my neighbor, Julia. I called her Jules, for short. We would dig for worms, go fishing down at Tinicum if we could get someone to drive us, play mini golf, or go to movies. She was ok. She was always up for an adventure. It just would have been a lot cooler to hang out with her if she wasn't a girl. Like when we would play "Stretch Armstrong" at her house, she always made me go first, and then quit. The game is, you pull your pants down, including underwear, and see how far you can try to touch your ball sack to your head.

She liked to rip worms in half and dare me to eat them. "If we both eat half at the same time, it's like we're married." She always said weird stuff like that, about marriage, and weddings, and friends forever. That's when I wished she were a guy. On my tenth birthday she tried to kiss me. We were standing on the dining room chairs, so that I was tall enough to blow out the candles on the cake, when she went for it. I saw it coming and tried to dodge it, which tripped up my feet and sent me hurdling towards the ground. It was a disaster. Everything kind of shifted into slow motion for the brief second that I was in flight. I fell forward, landed balls-first on the corner of the coffee table, sliced my arm on the cake knife, and collapsed to the ground. The party abruptly ended with me squirting blood and screaming myself hoarse from the most impossible testicular pain ever felt.

Then life, in one of its incredibly rare moods, shifted in my favor. Right at the end of the school year, Kyle Hall's family moved in next door.

They came from somewhere in northeast Philly, Kyle told me. I first met him running over a plate of *Welcome to the Neighborhood* cookies with a Hallmark card and some flowers from our garden out back. Grandmom made me do it. She always made me deliver stupid stuff around the neighborhood.

Kyle was cool. He was exciting and audacious, and always invited me to partner up on his explorations of the neighborhood. Mostly, we caused trouble. We broke into garages, busted the locks on the church windows so we could climb in and run around in between the pews, bang on the organ, and rearrange the service pamphlets. On more mundane afternoons, we chucked rocks through our neighbor's windows, pedaling off at top speed on our BMX bikes, laughing our heads off. Kyle was the counterpart I'd been missing all my life; we were instantly ten-year-old, mischievous, best friends.

Nothing beat the end of June when the corner stores would start to sell poppers, those little white tissue paper pellets that make a loud *crack* noise when they explode, for the 4th of July. They were the greatest, and we always stockpiled. We'd throw them at cars passing by, diving for cover in the bushes whenever someone pulled over to yell at us. One time the old geezer from Valley Road screeched to a stop and chased us down on foot, hollering how far up our ass he was going to jam his boot if we ever did that again. We laughed about that for weeks.

On the rare cloudless nights of early summer, we would walk through the neighborhood barefoot, to callous up and wear in our "summer feet." There were three blocks of houses to the east where the streets were clean enough to walk down without cutting our toes on broken glass; we circled them for hours, in a crude figure-eight pattern, talking about life and how we were going to conquer it.

"Have you ever seen a double decker?" Kyle asked.

"No." I said.

"I saw it in Scouts magazine. It's a tree house with two floors, and the only way to get up is to climb skinny vines on the outside of the first floor. If you fall, you break your legs. I did it once."

Kyle was big into Boy Scouts. He was always going on about the medals they'd earn, and the challenges they'd win, and the camping trips they'd go on. I never saw the appeal. The kids in Boy Scouts were weird. Hiking out into the middle of nowhere to purposely strand yourself for days, surviving on berries and whittling sticks together for forty minutes before you can make a fire just so you can fry up the two ratty Sunfish you caught earlier that day after six hours of fishing with a group of kids who think Dungeons and Dragons is still a cool game, wasn't for me. But Kyle loved it, and he ended up teaching me everything he learned, so I might as well have been a scout.

"Where'd you do that?" I asked.

"Billy from my troop had one. He lives in a mansion with his Dad. His tree house had a TV in it."

"That's awesome." I said. I was imagining a palace in the sky; couches, shaggy orange carpets, video games, and an everlasting supply of candy. Swedish Fish, of course. "We should make a double decker, too."

"We can't."

"Probably a lot of money," I said, thinking out loud.

"And a lot of wood. We don't need that much. The big tree out back will be perfect for our house."

Every morning, from the first day of summer until that dreaded last night of freedom, Kyle and I met high up in the branches of the old pine tree out back. The old thing doubled as an unofficial dividing line between our adjacent backyards, and our super-official hideout.

There was a moldy, termite-infested, wooden fence at the base of the trunk that served as a step-ladder to reach the first branch of the tree which seemed to be a good twenty feet up at the time, but was more likely only around six. From there, the thick branches formed a spiral stairway up to our base camp; three even branches comprised the floor, and the view from a small clearing let us keep watch over the backyards of all the houses as far as three plots down the block. We didn't even need to build anything, it was already perfect. I remember we were level with the top of the second story windows of my house, and often climbed much higher.

Our mortal enemy was always my Grandmother, doing laundry

on the second floor, right there level with our fort in the old pine. She hated that we climbed up that high, and she always made a fuss about it. Granddad worked pretty long hours as a house painter, so it was mostly just Grandmom taking care of me during the week. In the summer I drove her nearly mad day after day, but in my defense, it wasn't even my fault. She never had any idea what was going on. She didn't understand computers, or the internet, or simple things like AOL Instant Messenger (AIM). We fought a lot about it. I never met my dad, but Granddad always said I got my temper from him.

My mother and father died when I was eight months old. It was their first official "date night" since I had been born, and my grandparents had volunteered to babysit so they could get out for a few hours. Their car was hit head-on by some hipster, stoned out of his mind, trying to enter the highway via the exit ramp. Everyone was killed.

A big, framed photo of the two of them on their last date night sat in our living room on top of the china cabinet. Mom was wearing a black dress with flats, and my dad donned khakis with a blue blazer. They looked good, all things considered; it was the 80's, looking good was not an easy feat. Grandmom kissed their photo every morning while she made her tea. I didn't like to look at it. It only reminded me that I would never meet my mom and dad, never get to know who they were or hear them laugh or watch them argue the way everyone else at school could do with their parents. I understood life wasn't fair, but why couldn't it be unfair in my favor?

My grandparents took custody of me after they died. Grandmom and Granddad were all I'd ever known for parents, and I loved them to death, but Jesus Christ they knew nothing about technology, or computers, or cell phones, or being young, or about anything else in the world. Every time I was doing something important online, for example: talking to Kyle on AIM, Grandmom would pick up the dumbass phone and disconnect the internet like a moron to call one of her nutty friends to talk about Baked Alaska recipes and bird feed.

Sometimes I exploded. I don't know what it was exactly that would "click" and make me lose my temper; there was no rhyme or reason to it, it was just… bad. Sometimes big things would trigger it, like not being able to stay out past the streetlights coming on. Other times, if we ran out of milk, or my Granddad bought the wrong brand of waffles, I would flip. I spent hours, days, weeks in therapy with the great douche Dr. Goldstein, who doused himself in so much Ralph Lauren *Polo Black* cologne I still, to this day, cannot hold a conversation with someone wearing it without visibly gagging. He was always trying to "find the solution." He'd repeat that line, "*We must find the solution!*" about a hundred times a session, as if it would get me to magically expel the precise medical breakdown of my clear and present mental illness.

I didn't have a fucking mental illness, I was just a pissed off ten year old who wanted desperately to hang out with his dead parents.

Stupid Dr. Goldstein with his hair, pure white as the driven snow, and his eyebrows, thicker than Granddad's entire beard, pissed me off more than anything my grandparents could have ever done. I would transform into a blind fit of uncensored rage, screaming *fuck this* and *fuck you*; running out of his offices into the streets, causing a scene for all of the other kids to see. I guess I wanted the attention, and being a little pain in the ass was my way of getting it. Any adult with half a brain could see my true issues, but not Dr. Goldstein. Not while Grandmom was still writing him checks. "*…No solution in the foreseeable future, but we are trying a new theory… just a few more weeks, I'm sure of it…*"

CHAPTER SIX

That first summer, when Kyle and I discovered the old pine tree that became our fortress, my Grandmother went on what we forever called "Ground Mode." She grounded me every other day. It was the most annoying thing in the world. For the first few weeks I would have to come inside, sit in my room, and *think about what I'd done* until dinner. When my behavior worsened, so did the punishments, and I wouldn't be allowed outside for days.

During groundings I would sneak into the basement and play Duke Nukem on our computer. Our house was originally an apartment complex, so there were two separate stairways running from the third floor to the basement, which made it easy to get around under Grandmom's radar. The problem was, the wooden stairs were narrow, but loud and creaky, while the carpeted side was quiet, but much more exposed. After countless failures, I finally graduated to the expert ninja level necessary to make it around the house unnoticed.

I'm not bragging, I lost half of my summer to the basement, but I beat Duke Nukem, which was an extremely proud moment.

With little to do having conquered the only game we owned, I stumbled on the cheat codes to make the strippers in the video game flash their tits. I'm not sure I understood what was so good about it at the time, I just knew it was against the rules and I liked it. That's one habit that has never died.

The absolute worst grounding was having to go to our local pool with Grandmom and her old-as-dirt friends who sat in the shade the whole time and played near-extinct card games like Hearts. It was torture.

"Why do you want to go to the pool all of the time if you're not even going to get in the water?" I'd shout. I would always mouth off, followed by a short temper tantrum such as pulling down a bunch of books from the bookshelf, or kicking over the umbrella stand.

The reason I hated going to the pool was because I didn't know any of the other kids my age, so I had no one to hang out with. We had all just started middle school, and all of the elementary schools had been awkwardly thrown together into one big jumbled mass of confusion. All of the kids at our pool, Towertop Swim Club, were from Cynnewood Elementary. I was from Statham Park Elementary, which was on the other side of town. When you're ten years old, things like these are a huge deal, and at the time I wasn't very good at meshing with others. Going to the pool was never much fun.

My Grandmother referred to my behavior as "socially retarded" a lot because it made all of her bat-eyed, undead friends chuckle. I preferred to describe it as *an unwillingness to conform* to an inferior type of being. I didn't like to play basketball, which is all the Cynnewood kids did. I didn't like to do front-flips and backflips off the diving boards, or harass the lifeguards until I got benched. I was quiet and weird; I liked to swim underwater with my goggles strapped and pretend I was a seal, twisting and turning and darting around like seals do. You can see why there was a disconnect.

Jules went to Towertop, too.

"Hey Tyler! Come to the snack bar with me," she said, sitting down right next to me on the edge of the pool. It was adult swim, and I was dangling my feet in the water waiting for the whistle to blow again.

"Um, I dunno…" I said. There was a multitude of reasons why I didn't want to go. First, I really wanted to get back in the water, and there weren't even any adults swimming in the stupid pool so I don't know why the heck they decided to call an adult swim. Second, Jules hung out with a lot of her sister Lindsey's friends, and they were all sixteen and crazy. Not to mention, Grandmom rarely ever gave me snack bar money, so I would just be sitting there surrounded by a million girls talking about gymnastics, or horses, or whatever, without a snack.

"Come on! There's still ten minutes of adult swim left. My mom gave me three bucks, we can split it," she said.

Three bucks was a lot. Like four water ices. Or two water ices and fifteen airheads, or two large chipwiches, or just thirty airheads. White airheads were the best. Then light green.

She grabbed my arm and yanked me up. I guess I had no choice.

"How's your Grandmom?" she asked.

"She's ok," I said.

"Can I come over for dinner?"

"Yeah."

Jules's family lived next door to the Halls, which was essentially next door to me. Both her parents worked, so a couple nights a week she would come over after school and we would hang out. We played a lot of Duke Nukem in the basement, at least until I beat it. I would aim, she would shoot. She was actually pretty good.

"Hey Tyler?"

"What…"

"Do you like me?"

"Yeah."

"How much?"

"I dunno… a lot, I guess," I said. She was always asking weird questions.

"Good, because I like you too." She grabbed my hand and pulled me along. "Race you to the snack bar!"

She only beat me because she cheated, so I made her get us bomb pops and seven airheads, all white flavor. They blew the whistle, which meant adult swim was finally over, and we went back in the water. I taught Jules how to do a double-spin underwater that day.

Kyle got to come to the pool as a guest a few times, which were always the best days of the summer. Inviting guests could get expensive, and Grandmom was on the cheap side about things like that (surprise), but every first Thursday of the month was Tube Night where guests could come for free. There were a limited number of kids that could attend, and it was first-come, first-serve on the signup sheet. "Kyle Hall" was always the first name on that list. I made sure of it.

Kyle didn't belong to a pool, and his father sure as hell had no plans for that to ever change. Mr. Hall was a strange guy. I always did my best to avoid interacting with him. His hair was always a mess, and he bummed around unshaven in one of three totally stained, button-down shirts, regardless of what day of the week it was. He claimed to be a pediatric nurse at the UPenn hospital downtown, and would head into Center City seven days a week. This of course was a lie. He went downtown to drown himself at the pub.

I never met Kyle's mother. She was gone before I came

along. I think she's the reason they moved from the northeast.

You would have never known anything was wrong by looking at Kyle. He always had an upbeat attitude and was ready to take over the world, even while the real one around him crumbled.

His sister, Emma, was the most annoying girl on the face of the earth. Way worse than Jules. She was a fat little nuisance reminiscent of a potato with legs, and was always out to wreck a good time. At first she tried to join our games, but Kyle wouldn't let her. She was a girl, and she was fat and slow, so the decision was made final early on. In spite, she enabled a seriously intense level of what all men know as "being a huge bitch," constantly tattling on us, and stealing our bike locks so we couldn't ride anywhere.

"How long can you hold your breath?" Kyle asked.

"The length of the whole pool," I said. We were out on Kyle's back patio eating ice pops in the humid heat of late July.

"Really? Wow. Ok." He crunched down on the last chunk of his lime-green pop. "So here's the plan. We have three main targets to hit: the deep end, the five-foot side, and the snack bar." I nodded in agreement. "The deep end is cool, but only for like ten minutes until your ears start to pop from being at the bottom for so long," he said.

I knew for a fact Kyle had never touched the bottom of the deep end. I saw him try for it a few times, but I don't think he ever learned how to swim. He'd only get about five feet down before frantically turning back. He swam like a drowning deer, it was hilarious. I'd always turn my head when he came back up and pretend like I didn't see anything. I didn't want to embarrass him.

"So we should mostly hang out in the five-foot," he said.

"Ok."

"And adult swim is every half hour?"

"Every forty-five minutes."

"Ok. One minute before they blow the whistles, we'll head to the snack bar. We'll be first in line. We'll repeat the process every hour. This will be perfect!" Adventures were spur of the moment, but Kyle always insisted events like Tube Night be meticulously planned out. "Everyone will be jealous of us. The girls especially."

I loved Tube Night because for once I didn't care about what other people thought of me. I wasn't bothered by the Cynnewood kids, and Grandmom left me alone. Tube Nights were the exact opposite of what it was like when I went to the pool alone; I spent Tube Nights with my best friend.

"Hey guys!" The back door swung open. Barely squeezing through the frame was fat ass Emma.

"Shouldn't you be in a buffet line somewhere?" Kyle asked. I cracked up.

"I brought you guys some more ice pops," she said, cheerfully handing me a blue one. "Do you want to see my drawing?" she asked Kyle.

"No, go away."

She ignored him and flipped through her drawing notebook to a sketch of a little boy and a girl sitting on two rocking chairs, overlooking a small farm. It was drawn in colored pencil, vibrant in color without being too obnoxious, and well proportioned. It was really quite good.

"It's me and you," she said. She stood tall, proudly, but couldn't stop from tapping her foot nervously. You could tell she was waiting for Kyle's reaction, yearning for his approval.

"Wow…" Kyle said, biting open the top of his new freeze pop. "What a piece of shit."

I could almost see her little heart shatter into a million pieces. Kyle was laughing in his evil-villain cackle that he does sometimes. Usually it's hilarious, but this time I couldn't find it in me to laugh. I felt terrible for her.

"...I made it for you," she said, fighting tears.

"Thanks, I'll be sure to display it with the rest of the garbage—in the dumpster."

She clutched the drawing to her chest with both arms, sniffling.

"Emma, *go away*. Seriously. We have work to do," he said, kicking one of the empty chairs at her. She turned and ran off. I wished I would have told her I liked her drawing.

With no father figures going out of their way to give us "the sex talk," Kyle and I had to figure a lot out on our own. His dad was never around, and when he was, he was drunk. My grandfather was old-school, and probably figured I'd ask him about it on my eighteenth birthday as I shipped off to the war.

The reality of a public school education in Philly is that you learn about sex in second grade, at around seven or eight years old. I might not have been old enough to act on it, but I certainly knew what it was. Now I was eleven; I'd been around sex for years. The pressure to make something happen was growing more and more real. I had maintained a girlfriend for a solid two months in fifth grade, but it was short lived, and we didn't even kiss. That needed to change.

My sex education came directly from porno mags. Kyle somehow talked our neighbor into selling him a few mags, and so we started our research project—trading off magazines every other day or two. We'd meet up and discuss what we had learned and, having read the issues from front to back, there was always much to review.

"When we're at school, we need to make sure we do what the guys in the articles do," Kyle said.

"Ok," I said, shifting my weight to the branch a few inches above my normal spot.

"So, basically, did you read the part about the box?"

"Yeah."

"I think that's a good strategy. The alphabet trick is easy to remember," he said. I couldn't remember what the box was, so I changed the subject.

"We should probably start with trying to unhook their bra," I said. "They said that's a tricky part."

"Yeah, I saw that too," he said, his brow furrowed in thought. "I wonder if Lindsey would let us practice on her."

We both cracked up. Last Friday night Lindsey's parents went away and she threw a big house party, and Kyle and I tried to get a look at what was happening from his roof. We climbed out of the attic window and shimmied across the shingles, perching one floor up from her bedroom window. She was a little promiscuous and fooled around with a lot of older guys, and a few weekends before, Kyle and I saw her with some guy up in her bedroom. It would have been a great spot for spectating, but her bed was a few feet to the left of the window and always out of sight by the time anything good got going. It was heartbreaking; the anticipation…the letdown.

We were hoping things would be different this time. The party looked pretty crazy from where we sat; a couple was making out on the lawn in the backyard, and some dude barfed out of the second story window onto the windshield of her mom's van.

The light flicked on in Lindsey's room.

"Yes!" Kyle said.

"Is it her?" I asked. It was too far to tell, and Kyle had the binoculars.

"Yeah it's her!" He passed me the nocs. I focused in and saw Lindsay and some football jock hooking up, standing in the middle of the room.

"Oh shit, he's about to cop a feel!" I said. This was the best.

"Let me see," Kyle grabbed the binoculars from me. "Oh my God, she has some huge tits--"

"Kyle?"

My heart skipped a beat. It was a woman's voice from somewhere down below. I slowly laid down against the roof, hoping I would blend in.

"Kyle Hall is that you? Who else is up there?" It was Jules. *Shit.* She was taking out the trash and she spotted us.

"Oh, hey Jules." Kyle said, as nonchalantly as possible.

"Are those binocu…" she looked up to her sister's window, putting two and two together. "Gross, Kyle! You're such a creep."

"Whatever. It's not what it looks like."

"So you're *not* spying on my sister right now? Because that's what you were doing the last three times we caught you on your roof with binoculars."

I stifled a laugh. I didn't know Kyle had been caught before.

"Who else is up there with you?"

"Tyl--"

"Shut up!" I punched him. I was trying to stay hidden. I was just about perfectly camouflaged laying against the black shingles in my white t-shirt.

"Tyler?" Jules said. *Damnit.* I sat up and ashamedly said hi. "Why didn't you just call me, Tyler? You could have come over to the party with me," she said.

"*Yeah Ty, why didn't you just call her?* We could have gone to the party!" Kyle said, mocking Jules.

"Not you, Kyle. Never you. Just Tyler."

Burn. Jules tossed the trash bag of beer cans into the garbage bin and went back inside. "See you tomorrow, Tyler."

There was a moment of silence, then the light clicked off in Lindsey's room, and we couldn't see anything. We'd missed the whole show.

"Jules is such a bitch," Kyle said.

"She's not that bad..."

"She is. She's always trying to sabotage things. Like tonight."

"What 'things'?"

"With me and Lindsey."

"...I'm pretty sure Lindsey hates you." She did. With a passion. Lindsey was always really nice to me when I saw her around town, mostly because I had to hang out with Jules a lot, but she absolutely despised Kyle from the minute he moved in. Probably because he peeped on her so much. Clearly the whole Levin family has caught Kyle looking more than a few times.

"She has small tits anyway," he said, heading back inside. That was the last time we peeped on Lindsey together.

I thought about Jules. Next time I would probably call her, like she said I should. Those parties looked cool.

"I guess Lindsey letting us unhook her bra is probably out," Kyle said. We both took a moment, staring blankly in thought.

"How about your sister?" I asked.

"What the fuck?"

"I mean like, we could just grab one from the laundry to see how it works."

"Grab one of your Grandmom's then. That's gross, dude. I'm not doing that."

"No, I didn't...never mind. I didn't mean it like that." I snapped a couple twigs off of the branch I was sitting on, averting my eyes.

"It's easy, anyway. I've seen Lindsey do it a million times already," he said. "Every night, around 9:30 she gets naked. I watch the whole thing from the roof." He had the biggest smirk.

"Every night?"

"Every night," he said, proudly. And that's exactly why the Levin family hated him.

"Thanks for the invite." I said. "I don't even know what the back of a bra looks like."

"There's just a little latch that connects the straps."

"How many straps?"

"I don't know, probably two," he said. "Worse comes to worst, you can just rip it off."

I thought about it. Seemed legit.

"Before that though, we have to figure out how to make out with them. A lot of the time they'll take the lead and you'll end up getting mad head," he said.

"Which article did that happen in?" I asked.

"I looked it up online. If you unhook her bra the right way, she'll probably suck your dick."

CHAPTER SEVEN

"He wasn't a misogynistic asshole," Rachel said.

"So you *do* know him," I said.

"I want to know about what happened to you and Kyle and Jules in 2002. You were all sixteen. I don't care about how you guys popped boners together when you were ten."

"Eleven, if you were listening."

"Do you think this is a game?"

"No. This is my life you're threatening, remember?" I said. She picked up her cell phone and started punching in a few numbers. "What are you doing?" I rose from my seat.

"Calling my lawyer," she said.

"Wait! Wait! Wait! I thought we had a deal?"

She just looked at me, tapping in more numbers on her phone.

"I'll tell you about 2002, I swear." I took a deep breath. "But if you want to understand how it happened—how I worked my ass off for *years* to become an 'overnight success' as you've so pertinently described, touring the world, exploring new countries and continents with privileges few humans have ever acquired… only to make the mistake of bringing *you* up to my hotel room—

you have to understand how it all started. Now, please hang up the fucking phone."

She stopped. Smiled. "Good," she said, putting down the phone. "This is going to be quite the story."

I let out a frustrated grunt and turned back towards the window. My head was killing me. I needed another drink. "Can we at least order up another bottle of champagne?" I asked. She picked up her phone again. "Ok, calm down. Got it..."

Blackmail was taxing.

CHAPTER EIGHT

The Christmas before my thirteenth birthday, Kyle and I both received acoustic guitars. It was an unexpected present for me; my grandparents were notoriously bad gift-givers. I had figured I'd get the usual, some gift shop trinket or free giveaway from the department store…they did what they could, I guess.

I had never expressed interest in playing guitar, but my grandparents had noticed my recent obsession with the band Nirvana, and must've decided to give it a shot. I guess it was a positive alternative from running around town wreaking terror on the neighborhood; Kyle and I had earned a dark and notorious reputation. I think they were getting worried and somewhat desperate for ideas on how to fix my problems.

Every year I mostly looked forward to Jules's present. We would meet up Christmas day in the back corner where the corner of our yards touched and exchange gifts over the fence. Sometimes I'd give her comic books, or video game posters, which she always said she loved. Last year I stole a pair of earrings for her from the Claire's store on South Street. She wore them every day at school for the entire month of January, but she didn't tell anyone they were from me. It was our little secret thing.

Her gifts were amazing. She was the best gift-buyer ever, always putting my grandparents to total shame. She got me Age of Empires II last year, and an Airsoft KWC Taurus PT92 BB-gun this one. I didn't show it to Grandmom because I knew she'd take it away, but it came with these heavy-gauge metal pellets that Granddad showed me how to load, and that morning I shot a bird out of the Holly tree. Nailed it right in the throat. I'd never felt so horrible in my life. Jules jumped the fence and we both tried to save it, but it was a bloody mess because I'd shot clean through and broken its neck, so there was no hope. We dug a hole and buried him that afternoon. Poor little George, he didn't deserve to die.

Summer came soon enough, and that year Kyle and I decided we'd change our hangout spot from the pine tree out back to Kyle's front porch. We were both determined to become masters of our instruments, and a little friendly competition expedited that process from what normally may have taken years, to a matter of months. We practiced together every night. Every single night. Song after song, album after album. Nirvana's *MTV: Unplugged* album changed our lives, and after we had mastered it, we were inspired to write our own songs. Kyle was always roused by the discovery of a new band or an unreleased song or leaked B-side of an album, which in turn motivated me.

That's when I fell in love with music. Cool summer nights walking to his house in my bare feet, jamming out on that rickety old porch for hours on end. It was the first time I experienced that "blackout" feeling, where you forget where you are and just lose yourself in the music. Kyle and I were both what I like to call "repeat listeners." We would listen to the same song over and over and over and over and never get sick of it. It drove my grandparents mad. We did the same thing with playing guitar; one song, over and over, from around 8:00 p.m. when the sun would drop till maybe midnight, or whenever Mr. Hall would stumble home.

Other nights, I'd hear my Granddad yell for me from around the corner, which meant I was late and had better get my ass home right that second.

One night in early June, Mr. Hall ruined a really great jam session we had going. His bomber van came sputtering down the street blasting country music, shooting big puffs of black smoke out of its tailpipe. He always adopted a country slang to his talk when he came back from "work" which was weird. Kyle's whole family was from Philadelphia, to the best of my knowledge.

Mr. Hall tripped on the curb on his way to the porch.

"*Sniper!*" Kyle whispered to me. We both busted up laughing. He hated his father.

"What're you two boys still doin' up?" Mr. Hall snapped. It was around 11:30 p.m. "Well? What're you doin'?"

"What does it look like?" Kyle said.

"Watch it, Kyle."

He fumbled with his keys, holding the screen door open with his right foot. I dropped my eyes to the floor and started kicking around an acorn. This wasn't the first time Kyle fought with his dad. I hated when Mr. Hall came around. He scared the hell out of me.

"It's not locked," Kyle said.

"You say sum'n?" He turned and took a step towards Kyle.

Mr. Hall's eyes always struggled with low light, but once they connected, they locked on with unmatched ferocity. Sometimes when he looked at Kyle, you could actually *feel* the hatred; it was like he wanted to watch Kyle die. Just burn him at the stake right there. I'd never seen two men absolutely resent one another as much as Kyle and his dad.

Mr. Hall never looked at me, thankfully. I would have crumbled to ash the minute he glanced in my general direction. I counted my blessings.

"I said it's not even locked," Kyle said.

Mr. Hall heaved and kicked the door open, splintering the door handle. Whether it was locked or not made no difference now.

"Git inside! Right now. Git yer ass to bed."

Kyle stood up violently, knocking his chair over.

"And where's your sister?" Mr. Hall asked.

Kyle's countenance changed whenever that question was raised. As often as he made fun of Emma, he had her back, and wasn't about to let his father near her. Kyle really loved her.

He silently grabbed his guitar and walked inside.

I knew things would only get worse and I sure as hell wasn't going to stick it out on the porch alone with Mr. Hall; I saw my opportunity and took it. I bolted off the porch with my guitar and didn't look back.

But despite the occasional bad ending to a night, our jam sessions always started back up the next day from right where we left off. We had important things to focus on: summer camp.

It was all Kyle's idea. He had brought over a brochure for a summer camp program called *Camp Innabah* that he'd picked up the day before at *Cenzo's*, the best pizza shop in town.

To be honest, the brochure didn't sell it too well. There was an under-exposed picture of a group of smiling kids running through a field, another amateur shot of camp counselors wearing tie-dyed t-shirts, happily helping a bunch of five year olds glue beads to construction paper, and a pool, all superimposed with crummy Microsoft *WordArt* and way too many exclamation points!!!

But by Kyle's description, you would have thought he was holding a golden ticket to Wonka's factory.

"Dude, Tyler, I found it." He said. I had my bike flipped upside down and was trying to get the chain back onto the only gear it had.

"Found what?" I asked.

"The adventure of a lifetime; the perfect way for us to get our music heard and find girlfriends." He was elated.

"Yeah, right," I said, frustrated with my bike. He stuck the brochure in front of my nose.

"Camp Innabah... girls from everywhere around the country drive hundreds of miles to go to this camp for the week, to escape their crappy lives in hopes of finding a better one here."

"That's why you want to go?" I asked.

"These girls are dying to meet new guys! Why *wouldn't* we go?"

He had a point.

"How do you know?" I asked.

Kyle pointed to a photo of one of the counselors wearing a bikini. "What more proof do you need? This is it! This is our ticket to having sex with girls."

I was sold.

We planned out how we would sell it to my grandparents, and to Kyle's dad. Two completely different beasts, but we knew we could tame them both. It was four hundred dollars for a week of glory, freedom, and potential debauchery that we were not going to miss. There was no room for failure.

That night I asked Granddad and Grandmom if I could go to camp with Kyle. I gave them a long-winded, dramatic proposal with as much detail as I could remember from Kyle's original pitch, minus the sex part. It was a tough sell. Grandmom wouldn't stop nudging Granddad and whispering "*Look Lenny, he's so adorable!*" right in the middle of my presentation, which kept throwing off my train of thought and forcing me to re-start at the last bullet point, but overall I think the flow of the pitch was decent. I think Grandmom was mostly impressed with my enthusiasm. Granddad asked a few questions, like how long it was and how far away, which I explained to him in vast, overly descriptive detail. He gave a few grunts of approval, sipping his tumbler of scotch.

I guess the campgrounds were close enough and my proposal was at least somewhat convincing, because they said I could sign up for camp in the morning. I gave them ferocious hugs and ran off to my room like a little girl, screaming with delight in this weird opera-style soprano voice that I sometimes do when I'm ecstatic.

"It doesn't concern you when he does that? The boy sounds like a woman."

"Oh hush, Leonard."

CHAPTER NINE

Camp started on Saturday. We drove about an hour and a half into northwestern PA to a small town called Spring City, and pulled our car into the dusty gravel parking lot alongside the other families. The butterflies in my stomach nearly killed me, daydreaming about possibilities of what could happen as soon as I set foot on the lot. I had it all played out perfectly in my mind: two cute girls would come up to Kyle and I, take our hands, and lead us away into abandoned cabins to make out. Possibly even sex. I was all riled up just thinking about it.

There were multiple camps that went on during the week, so it was impossible to determine who was attending which program just by looking at them in the parking lot, which multiplied the suspense by about a million percent. Every cute girl stopped my heart; every handsome competitor filled it with lead. I hated every guy my age as soon as I set eyes on him. I was not going to let this camp turn into Towertop Swim Club.

I said my goodbyes to Granddad and Grandmom. Of course they both decided to come along to send me off, which meant we had to listen to Frank Sinatra the whole way up because Grandmom loves him and hates all other music. To make things worse, they had to take a hundred thousand pictures of me as I carried my sleeping bag from the car to the sign-in line ten feet away, and Grandmom nearly started crying when it came time for me to leave. I was ready to throw a fit, but decided against it for my reputation's sake. I kissed them both goodbye and trekked up to the cabins.

I needed to find Kyle.

Camp Innabah was the glorious American soil that introduced me to the completely illogical, spellbinding world of women. Tall, century-old pines littered the sky, outlining the grassy grounds, separating the lakes from the pathways to the cabins. A massive tepee tent held its own at the center of the largest field, providing a marker for the entrance to the campfire quarters, hidden away deep in the far corner of the woodlands. Alas, from that first week of camp on, women became the bane of my existence, and the core of my future music career. It all started here.

I found Kyle near the pool. His dad had already left. Kyle didn't want to walk up to the camp grounds; he insisted we ride up on one of the counselor's golf carts so we would "arrive like kings." I didn't care either way, so I waited with him for the cart.

"What happened to your eye?" I asked, pointing to his bruised right eye. Nothing huge, but noticeable.

"Got into a fight," he said.

I laughed out loud. "Yeah, right. What *actually* happened?"

"Restringing my guitar, my hand slipped and I smacked myself in the eye," he said.

"Not as good a story as the fight."

"I know."

We set up our bunks and joined the rest of the campers at the picnic tables at the top of the hill where we each introduced ourselves. By the looks of the competition, it was going to be a great week; Kyle and I were the top dogs.

The first girl I had a major crush on was named Kym and yes, it annoyed me how she spelled her name. She was a sporty English girl who wore Adidas shorts and tank tops and always had a little pep in her step. I loved it, her accent especially. Kyle wasn't lying; girls from all over the world *did* come to Camp Innabah.

Kym had me lost in a trance with her every move. It was then that I realized I was definitely one of those guys who is attracted to the exact opposite of himself; she was loud, openly opinionated, and loved to be the center of attention—polar to my personality.

The foundation of my relationship with Kym that week was built on curiosity; we both wanted to explore what it was like to be with the opposite sex. As the week progressed, we would hang out more and more. We'd eat dinner together, sit next to each other during the campfires, or even swim in the same general area of the pool when playing water-basketball.

Friday night was movie night in the rec room. It was a big night, and marked a significant countdown. It was either going to happen, or not; Kyle made sure to remind me every fucking half hour I saw him. Still, I took things slow with Kym. I wanted to treat her right so that on Friday night I could, God willing, unhook her bra.

Kyle was a little more…ambitious. He was occupied for most of that week trying to swoon a girl named Kate, who was a massive bitch. I don't know why he went after such impossible girls. Maybe it was because he liked the challenge.

We were at the pool before dinner on a particularly hot afternoon; Kyle was benched for doing backflips off the side of the pool in the shallow end, and I was in the deep end with

Kym diving for pennies. The minute he was de-benched by the lifeguard, Kyle ran over to Kate and gave her a crisp smack on the ass.

"Show me your tits!" he screamed, diving backwards into the pool, howling with laughter. I personally thought it was hilarious, which bought me a dirty look from Kym. The counselors and the lifeguard looked like they were going to hang Kyle from a tree when he came back up for air, so I dipped underwater to warn him.

Underwater he gave me the thumbs up sign, grinning ear to ear, then pretended to squeeze a pair of monstrous boobs and humped the floor of the pool like a dog. I nearly drowned of laughter and had to resurface, only to hear Kyle's evil cackle of a laugh cutting through the shouts from the angry mob of counselors, which he always did when he knew he was in irreconcilable trouble.

He swam to the opposite side of the pool and hopped out, just to further piss off the counselors who now had to walk around to the other side of the pool, and was met by a most furious Kate. She kicked him as hard as she could, square in the nut sack. His face went purple and he collapsed to his knees on the pool deck without a sound. I think his balls were lodged in his throat. Everyone fell silent for a moment, as Kyle faded unconscious.

Kate stormed off, and Kyle was carried off to the nurse's office. I didn't see him again until we all went to sleep that night.

"You alright?" I asked as he hobbled to his bunk.

"The worst blue balls, dude. You don't ever want this kind of blue balls," he groaned.

"Did you talk to Kate?"

"Yeah. She came by the hospital wing for a couple hours. She said she felt bad and wanted to make it up to me, so she let me feel her tits."

He always one-upped me.

On Friday night, Kym and I positioned ourselves next to each other on the floor of the rec room while the counselors passed around blankets and pillows. I wanted to get close, but not so close that I made my intent obvious, so I waited for a pair of pillows, plopped them down next to one another, and laid back. She followed my lead, and pulled a blanket over her legs. The lights dimmed and Varsay, the best counselor by far, popped *The Goonies* into the VHS player.

After what felt like forty-five minutes but was probably thirty seconds, I built up enough confidence to fake-shiver and asked if I could have some of her blanket. She obliged. My right leg lay bare next to her left, close enough so that they slightly touched, which felt so intimate I thought we'd maybe just had sex. My heart was slamming savagely up and down inside my chest so loud probably everyone in the room could hear. My breathing was short and choppy like a panting dog's, and I could feel myself sweating profusely. It was hot in that tiny room and the dumbass blanket I'd just asked to get under wasn't helping.

I changed my arm position, quickly uncrossing them, laying my right one out parallel to my torso, which caused me to accidentally brush my arm against hers and freak out even more. *I blew it. Oh God, I blew it and I knew it and that was it.* I could already see it:

"Eww get off me, creep!" she would scream, running to the counselors, pointing at me with tears in her eyes as I lay helpless in a pool of my own sweat. "That's him, that's the pervert who tried to attack me!"

Instead, she took my hand and let her fingers fall in between mine. My heart rate slowed. It stopped pounding. My sweating ceased, and I could breathe again. Slow and methodic, like a sniper at his scope. Her touch was warm and sensual. *She liked me. She* was holding *my* hand. This was a victory previously undiscovered in my book, and it felt incredible.

I didn't kiss Kym during the movie, but I still had time to make a move that night at the campfire. The counselors, led by Varsay, purposely wandered off to give everyone some "alone time," the greatest possible gesture a counselor could give. As the fire dimmed and the glowing embers illuminated the small out cove, I went for it.

The darkness was so thick I could barely see Kym next to me, let alone who else was still there, but I'm sure there were a few other couples fooling around. Kyle and Kate were sitting directly across from me, I remembered from earlier. I listened for his voice, but heard nothing. He was probably already banging Kate, or boxing her, at least. Everyone now and then someone giggled, but their whispers quickly fell silent to the chorus of locusts vibrating in the trees and the sizzling fire.

"Tyler," Kym whispered. Her voice was so sweet and calm, it melted me. "Do you want to kiss me?"

I gulped hard. *Showtime.* "Yes," I choked out.

"Ok," she said, lifting her leg over so that she straddled the bench, facing me. *Oh my God, this was it.* If I ever thought it was before, I was wrong, because this was most definitely it.

I tried to act smooth like I had done this before. Channeled my inner Gosling, but quickly realized that was a lost cause, which killed my already dwindling confidence even more. I tried to focus on the dorky kids at camp, and imagine how much worse they would screw this situation up if they were here. That did the trick.

I figured it best not to do exactly what she had just done and straddle the bench, so I weighed out my options, which were few, and decided not to move at all. I realized too late that I totally should have made some sort of movement, signaling that I was, in fact, interested in kissing her, but there was no going back now. I sat. Like a deer caught in headlights, I sat, frozen.

Kym took the reins. She had probably done this a few times before. *Definitely.* Hopefully with just one guy though, not like twenty. That would be sick—to kiss a girl who had already kissed like nine hundred other dudes.

Knees weak, arms heavy, I continued to just sit there.

Then she grabbed my shirt, right near my collarbone with an unexpected quickness, and pulled me in, slowly pressing against me, touching her lips to mine. Excitement and ecstasy flooded my body from head to toe, like lightning through my veins.

We kissed for a while before she slowly pulled back. I opened my eyes to see her smile, and then she let out one of those giggles like I had heard earlier. I couldn't stop staring into her eyes, they were so beautiful, and also the only things I could really see in the dark. The moment was so perfect; the crackling fire, the cool summer air. I didn't want to be anywhere but here.

Then, to my surprise, I took over; I held her chin gently between my thumb and index finger and pulled her back in. Despite the overwhelming anxiety I'd suffered *before* our kiss, I felt more relaxed in that moment than I think I had ever been. A flow of confidence seeped in, surely having passed from her lips to mine, and things just… took off. I pulled her leg up on top of mine to bring her body closer. It felt so right, it was mesmerizing. Empowering. Her breathing grew heavy with my every touch, and we were pulsing back and forth, in and out in a perfect rhythm, pulling, writhing. I placed a shaky hand on her shirt by her waistline, and slowly started to move up. Inch by inch, I was almost to her breast. *Oh God, oh God, oh God.*

Then she grabbed my wrist. I must have jumped, because she sort of chuckled and pulled my hand back down to her bare stomach, placing my fingers by her waistline, this time *under* her shirt. She guided my hand up until I reached her bra, which she unsnapped. I wasn't sure to be happy or kind of mad that she didn't let me do it, but the thought immediately left my mind as soon as I felt her. I was in another world.

Just as she started to reach for my belt, Varsay came a-whistling back down the path with about forty flashlights in his hands. Everyone scrambled; twigs snapping left and right, tripping over rocks, smacking shins on the benches, and diving back to original seats in a desperate attempt to not get caught. Kym fixed her bra, pulled her leg down, and swiftly shifted back to her regular sitting position. She pulled my arm up over her shoulder and snuggled in.

"Aye! *Aye!* Lights out! Back to your bunks, let's go!" Varsay yelled, shining the light of a thousand suns directly into everyone's eyes. There was a low chorus of complaints and groans as we reluctantly made our way back to the cabins. Varsay had impeccable timing for ruining the moment.

CHAPTER TEN

In eighth grade, cliques began to form within the student body, and a sociological hierarchy was born. After two years of bouncing off of each other since the big merge, we had all figured out the type of people we liked, and perhaps more importantly, those we didn't.

Kyle and I didn't really have a clique; we were "floaters." If he hadn't moved in next door I don't know where I would have ended up. Maybe with Jules, but she was part of the "cool" clique because her sister, Lindsey, was a senior cheerleader at school and basically ran the place. By default, Jules inherited her reputation. She couldn't have been more opposite of her sister, but I guess no one else at school knew. She had a huge group of new friends after like the first two days. I'd see her all the time, hopping in and out of cars, giggling with her girlfriends. I was jealous, I'll admit it. As annoying and overly attached as she was, I missed hanging out with her.

There weren't many kids who shared Kyle and my interest in music who weren't super-dork band-camp kids, and we sure as hell weren't about to join band or orchestra, and we didn't vibe well with the sports kids either, despite the fact that I was on the soccer and wrestling teams, so we pretty much just stuck it out together. We had all the same classes, so we teamed up for group projects, got our work done and continued to live in our awesome, exclusively imaginative world, concocting our genius plans.

It had been a few years since we started playing guitar, and we were getting pretty good. I figured it was time for us to start recording the music we were writing so that we could eventually put out an album, just like Nirvana. It was never about making money, it was always just about enjoying the process, and that proud feeling that comes with an accomplishment as epic as an LP. I wanted to show the world we could do it. Plus, in a year or two, we would have a record deal and wouldn't have to bother with school. It was a win-win situation.

After a few weeks of blood, sweat, and tears mowing the lawn, dusting, scrubbing toilets, and taking out the trash for allowance money, I was ripping open the packaging of my new 4-track recorder. It was gold with a buffed lacquer finish, like a new car, and had a quarter inch input, an RCA out, and a headphones jack. You could only record one track at a time, but you could overdub and layer four tracks simultaneously. That meant we could record both guitars, a guitar solo, and vocal; or any combination. Sometimes just one guitar, vocals, bass, and drums.

I didn't leave the basement for weeks. Kyle came over every day after school to record. He never took an interest in the technical side of things, so I always engineered. I'd finally found something I could do better than him, and I worked hard to make sure I was the best I could be. You can learn from reading books, but nothing beats experience. I bought a cheap condenser microphone kit that came with two mics, and a small mixing board so I could run both microphones in, mix them, then output them to the 4-track as one track. My mixing was essentially trivial, because while the microphones came in as a stereo feed to the mixing board, it ran mono back out to the 4-track, so panning was worthless. But it made me feel good knowing I could mic the drum kit in multiple spots and, albeit mono, I was still getting a better sound out of the drums recording two tracks for the price of one.

We set our sights on finishing twelve songs for the album.

Mixing and mastering them down, recording them all on to fresh blank tapes, designing the album art, printing the album art, and assembling the final tapes took damn near the entire summer. We were going to *kill* the competition at camp that year; there was no doubt about it. We just needed a name for our band.

At first we wanted to go with *Pariah*, but that name had already been taken. Then Kyle came up with *Run of the Mill*. Something about it just felt right. A lot of times, band names have an embarrassing feel to them when you say them out loud—like when you first start out and have to tell people what you call yourselves. But not *Run of the Mill*. Never in my life did a band name feel so natural. It was perfect.

That winter I convinced Kyle to join the wrestling team. I was bored out of my mind, with no friends and no real interest in the sport itself, and Kyle never had anything to do after school because I was always off at practice, so I told him to check it out one afternoon. He'd seemed angrier than usual for the past few weeks, often mumbling derogatory things about his dad. I never pried much because Kyle didn't like to talk about it, but I figured they'd been fighting more than usual, and Kyle could use wrestling as an outlet for his aggression.

Maybe it was the reputation that came with the gig, or the cheerleaders that always hung around after practice, or just the inherent violence of the sport, I'm not quite sure, but he immediately fell in love with it and joined the team. Being only a weight class apart, we hung out in the same groups for most of practice, which was awesome.

Our JV team won most of our meets, but Kyle and I won every single one of our individual matches, so within a few weeks our egos had exploded and we were those obnoxious, arrogant fourteen year olds everyone hates. We talked a lot of shit, made fun of the kids we beat relentlessly, picked arguments, and started fights. It was a good time for the most part. Harmless pranks.

Other times Kyle would push things a little too far. He could be kinda vicious. His temper flared if someone pushed the right buttons. Having mistakenly let on obvious clues about his weak spot—making cracks about his absent mom—most guys could easily piss him off. Kyle would retaliate during practice when the coach wasn't looking, by "accidentally" dropping forty-five pound plates on their toes in the weight room, donkey-kicking them in the stomach while they did pushups, or blind-siding them with a fifteen pound sand-bag to the face in the locker room. Most guys quickly learned it wasn't worth provoking him.

At practice one time Kyle thought it would be hilarious to whip our teammates in the legs with the elastic-coated wire jump ropes we worked out with. So while the coach hit the locker room for a quick piss, Kyle stopped jumping rope and launched his attack.

"Hey, Crate!" he shouted to one of the homelier kids on the team we called Crate. He was scrawny, with a lot of scarring acne.

"Leave me alone, Kyle." Crate said, focused on his workout.

"What's the matter, bro?" Kyle grilled him.

"Seriously, go away dude," he said.

Crate had made a joke about Kyle a few days earlier when rumor spread that Kyle was still a virgin. Something about how *the only tits he's probably ever grabbed were his mom's, but wait, she left before he could even play with them.* Kyle was great at holding on to grudges, and he'd been itching for the chance to get back at Crate for a few days now.

He snapped the whip across Crate's leg.

"Ahhh!" Crate screamed, crumpling to the ground as Kyle howled with laughter. He whipped him a lot harder than I had expected.

"What the fuck is your problem?!"

"I heard you were talking shit," Kyle said. Crate's leg was beet red. "Anything else to say?"

"Yeah. Fuck you and your junkie mom."

That was the first time I saw Kyle's flip switch. His pupils went sharp, like small, malicious black dots. He stopped laughing. He took another swing with twice as much force as before. The thinly coated wire bit at Crate with a deafening *crack*; tearing the skin, making Crate bleed. This had become a legitimate lashing, like medieval times.

"I'm sorry? I can't hear you!" Kyle screamed over Crate's cries. "Were you trying to apologize?"

"Fuck you!" Crate screamed again. Kyle took a step back to wind up for another strike.

I had made my way towards the back of the gym, not looking to get involved. Our other teammates tried to ignore what was happening; Crate didn't have many friends. But Matt Ryan, one of the tougher kids on the team, had seen enough. He was one of the few guys Kyle never messed with, because he could lay Kyle out flat without so much as batting an eye.

He called Kyle out.

"Fuck do you think you're doing, Hall?" Matt yelled, silencing the room. The coach was still on his piss leave. Kyle stopped and turned.

"Teaching Crate a lesson in manners."

"And who gave you permission to do that?"

"I don't need permiss--"

"Crate's my little brother," Matt said, taking a step forward. "Grew up down the street. We've been like family for years. Our mothers were friends." Matt walked straight up to Kyle, face to face. "But you wouldn't know much about mothers, would you."

The room was completely quiet, it felt like the air had been sucked out of it, like a vacuum. The floor felt like it was trembling. Kyle's fists were clenched, but everyone, including myself, knew he wouldn't throw a punch at Matt.

Then Kyle's demeanor changed. I'm not sure if anyone else noticed it, but I certainly did. It was like his anger just… floated away. The switch was flipped back. He loosened his fists, and the darkness in his eyes disappeared. He rolled back from the balls of his feet to his heels, and slouched his shoulders. His vehemence died.

"What's the matter? Nothing to say?" Matt taunted.

"Take it easy, Matty boy. If you want my comeback so bad, go wipe it off your mom's face." The whole team was hollering at that one. Kyle turned his back to Matt and winked at me, smiling.

"I don't think so." Matt said, grabbing him by the back of his shirt, throwing him to the ground.

"Me and you, tomorrow before practice. Tennis courts—"

"What the hell is going on here?" Coach's voice cut through the silence. "Why have we stopped jumping rope?"

Kyle agreed to fight Matt. He didn't want to talk about it, he just told me he was doing it, and that was that. It was his battle, not mine, and with certain things there's no point in even attempting to talk Kyle out of them. He was even more stubborn than me. I told him I'd do my best to help with preparations for the funeral. Matt was going to crush him.

By the next day, the entire school was talking about it. Fights were an adrenaline rush to watch. I loved them. I had never been *in* a fight, which is probably why I liked watching them so much, because I experienced them all vicariously through the winner. Bets were made, and sides were taken. It was going to be a fun afternoon.

Kyle and I watched a few back yard fight videos on YouTube, and Googled some mixed martial arts moves as a crash course. You learn from those videos that your best option is to just close your eyes, and walk into the pit. You've either got it, or you don't. Size is pretty important in fights. Kimbo Slice won a lot of fights, but he was a big dude. Matt was a big dude, too.

At 2:22 p.m. the bell rang, and what looked like the entire middle school started the long, testosterone-fueled march to the green-top tennis courts. It was a bright and cloudless day. Snow crunched beneath our feet as Kyle and I walked in silence towards the ring. He was in his zone, staring blankly ahead, channeling his rage. Fights drew crowds of usually around a hundred kids or more, which unfortunately made it extremely obvious for neighbors and teachers to spot and call the cops to shut them down. They usually lasted all of one or two minutes max before the blue and whites wheeled up.

I didn't have a pep talk ready or any words of wisdom for Kyle, which I regretted, because I should have. That's what a good friend would have done. He was always the one encouraging *me* to push the boundaries; this vice a versa business was all new to me. I gave him an empty pat on the back, which I'm not sure he even noticed. He dropped his book bag on a snow bank and walked into the middle of the circle of cheering fourteen year olds without a word. I wished I had told him to be strong, to keep his hands up, to focus on defense as much as offense, *something*. I could have at least said *good fucking luck*. I was terrified for my own skin; sometimes the opposing entourages would fight. I was the only one *in* Kyle's entourage, and I didn't want to fight.

Not today. I had a lump in my throat the size of an apple and was hyperventilating like a gigantic pussy.

Kyle was ready, though. He was always ready. You could see it in the way he walked into that circle—fists clenched, his back slightly arched in the "come at me bro" stance. For a minute, Matt looked small in comparison. He may have been physically bigger, but Kyle had a hell of a lot of heart.

Kyle kicked it off with a quick jab that dropped Matt flat to the floor, shocking and firing up the crowd. I tried to suppress a proud smile. He let Matt get back up to his feet before going at him again, swinging two more times, landing another. Matt popped back, a solid shot to the ear, which almost knocked Kyle down. They both took a few steps back to re-assess, then they charged at each other, arms flailing with fury. In exhaustion Matt tackled Kyle to the ground, but Kyle was able to pull a reversal on him, and in seconds he was straddling Matt, pinning his arms to the ground with his knees, wailing on his face with both fists. I couldn't fucking believe my eyes. Kyle was pummeling Matt into the ground like it was nothing..

Then the cops showed up. The crowd bolted in every direction, some hopping fences, others diving over bushes and cutting through hedges, desperate to escape the wrath of the law. In the midst of the commotion someone pushed Kyle off of Matt, and they were both now stumbling to their feet trying to find a way out. I grabbed Kyle's backpack and we both booked it back towards the middle school. I don't think anyone got arrested that day.

From then on, the dynamic of the wrestling team changed. Kyle was the new leader, whether anyone liked it or not. He still tormented kids when he felt the urge, but the team ceased prodding him, so he didn't have much reason to fight.

Kyle had won.

CHAPTER ELEVEN

Our second summer at Camp Innabah was even more nefarious than the first. We knew the ropes, the flow, the activities, even the counselors. We made friends and kept our enemies close. We came fully prepared with our guitars, copies of our *Run of the Mill* debut album (cassette tapes with our logos taped on), and a freshly rehearsed live show.

My girl that summer was a pretty Italian named Jessica. She had brown hair and brown eyes and stood eye level with me at around six feet tall. The height thing bothered me, I felt emasculated. I liked petit girls, like Kym from last year. But what the hell, Jessica was one of the cuter girls in this year's troop and we really hit it off, so there was no need to act hastily. Besides, how do you know whether you like something or not when you've never tried it? She was upbeat, always laughing and poking fun and here to have a good time. I could tell camp was her week away from whatever mess she came from.

I don't know what I did right or what I did well, or maybe it was what I *didn't* do, but mid-way through the week this girl was in love with me. Every inch of me. Every stuttered word out of my mouth, every shifty-eyed glance I shot her way, she melted. She was obsessed. Every sarcastic remark I made was a knock-out hilarious joke. Reactions like that are contagious, and soon enough everyone at camp started to think I was the funny guy. Kyle and I hadn't even broken out our guitars yet.

Jessica was also more, um... *sexually advanced* than I was. I was a late bloomer. My high-pitched voice had only gone away a few months ago; so naturally, I was a little low on the totem pole of experience. I had kissed a girl, and I had grabbed a tit. I had done plenty of research, of course; between the old magazines Kyle and I swapped and my discovery of LimeWire, a rip off of Napster that allowed you to download videos, my knowledge and understanding had grown exponentially. I just wasn't very confident about it. Jessica was.

That week at camp things ran rather smoothly for me and Kyle. All of our usual ploys worked gloriously; stealing time with the girls we liked, sneaking off during free-time hours, dominating the extra-curricular activities like ultimate frisbee and kickball.

And kickball? Kickball was my time to shine. While most kids whiffed or bunted straight to the pitcher, I could drill that deflated piece of rubber thirty yards past the overweight outfielders, staring at the grass with their hands down their pants. I'd played soccer all my life. This was *my* house. The counselors even forced me to bat lefty. Made no difference.

Run of the Mill was my first legitimate success as a musician. The feeling of being loved and praised for what you've dreamt up and willed into fruition is both awesome and addicting, and at camp that summer I was bitten by the business bug. We sold our tapes for five dollars each, and sold every single one we brought with us. It was also my first experience performing live for an actual audience other than my grandparents and our annoyed neighbors.

The campfire on Wednesday night was always a combined event between all of Innabah's programs, so the two other camps running that week were forcibly added to the mental-destabilization process known as *singing around a campfire.* Thankfully, Varsay never took it as far as *Kum-Baya*; we usually rocked out to some 90's Sugar Ray song or Barenaked Ladies. He loved those guys.

Kyle had already asked if we could perform two songs at the end of the session, and Varsay had agreed. He was too good at persuading people sometimes. It made me mad in times like these, when I wished the counselors had just said no and I wouldn't have to go out there and play in front of fifty kids. But Kyle could sell salt to a slug. I let go of that hope.

"Fingers still hurt?" Kyle asked.

"A little. My callouses haven't come back all the way," I said.

"I'm going to drop out completely at the end of your solo--"

"What?"

"At the end, as you're building up with that one riff you always play. If I cut out, it'll sound sick."

"Yeah, but that part only sounds good when you're backing it up with the right chords," I said, *not* excited about this last minute tweak.

"It'll be awesome."

"…I don't want to."

"Ty, you'll be fine, man. This is our time to shine."

"We've never done it like that before! I don't want to mess it up."

"Nothing is changing; I'm just going to stop playing. You play the same thing you always do. Relax, man. You got this." Kyle really had to push me to test my own limits; although, I think a lot of the time he was so lost in his own glory quest that his motivation was coincidental. If I didn't want to budge, he lit a fire underneath my ass. One way or another, we were going to do it his way.

Before long, the sing-along concluded and everyone stood up to leave.

"Varsay!" Kyle shouted from a distance, holding his guitar out.

"Oh, shit…" Varsay said. He remembered. *Damnit*. "Hold on! Hold on everyone! We have one last song. Sit back down, please," he shouted over the crowd. The audience looked about as excited to watch us play as a man looks coughing for the doctor gripping his balls. "Kyle and Tyler are going to perform for us."

I grimaced and took a long breath. Kyle was already out there perched on his stool, tuning up his guitar, smiling to himself. I was always jealous of his confidence. He truly believed the world was missing out every second that they weren't in his presence. I would have *killed* for courage of that caliber.

Thankfully, I was only the rhythm guitarist. I sat hunched over in my seat like a wilting flower trying desperately to sink back into the ground, as Kyle belted out a screechy version of our songs "Heartbreaker" and "Can You Help Me". He wasn't the greatest singer in the world; his voice must have cracked a hundred times. Each time, I visibly winced. But did Kyle? Nah. He didn't even notice. He was an amazing songwriter—I mean *really* amazing; some of his songs were the foundation of my extremely successful career in music later on—but Jesus Christ, he was a shitty singer.

I slouched even lower, trying to focus on my upcoming guitar solo through the trembling nerves betraying my fingers. This was *not* the time to freeze up. I could feel Kyle's eyes burning into my skull. *Shit.*

And then that wonderful blanket of darkness covered my hunched frame, and I forgot that I was sitting in front of an audience of fifty people. I forgot about Kyle. I didn't care about impressing Jessica or the counselors, or anyone else. I just played. I let the music pour out from my soul, through my fingers, out into the night air. And I crushed it.

Friday night of that week was the night. The big, amazing, mind-blowing life-changer. Jessica was still hot and heavy off of Kyle and my performance on Wednesday at the campfire. Plus, earlier that afternoon I had caught the only two sunfish in the entire scummy lake, so I was feeling pretty good.

"Tyler, come here," Jessica said, quietly. The campfire sing-along was just starting, and Varsay had his guitar in his lap. As usual, my heart was pumping like a goddamn piston.

"Tonight, we talk about *Faith*. Now, I don't care what religion you come from, or whether you are an Atheist or a daily church-goer. This isn't about our differences; it's about our similarities..." Varsay rambled on. He could be quite the preacher when he wanted to be.

"Come closer," she whispered. She was wearing a low-cut blue top and tight little jean shorts that frayed at the edges; I had noticed on my walk up. I didn't dare look at her now, I was so nervous, but I had her envisioned in my mind, like an artist right before painting that first stroke. I slid over, and our legs touched. I was wearing mesh shorts, which was the worst fucking choice in the history of choices ever made.

"Do you have a boyfriend?" I asked. I wanted to smack myself. *Such a dumbass.* Why the hell did I just ask that? It had been on my mind all week, despite the fact that I had kissed her on the second day of camp, but I'd never known for sure and clearly it was bothering me.

"No," she said. "...Do you have a girlfriend?"

"No."

"Well, good," she said.

Silence whirled around us. Seconds felt like hours. The fire flickered in slow motion. Varsay was singing his heart out up front, but I couldn't hear a damn thing. All I could hear was my sledgehammer of a heart convulsing beneath my ribs, and the little voice in my head mimicking *"do you have a boyfriend?"* over and over like an idiot. I was losing my mind.

Her hand touched my leg, gripping it. It wasn't a firm grip; it was the light, delicate touch of her palm to my knee, right at the edge of my shorts. I tried to control my breathing, but I couldn't concentrate on so much at once. It was either the breathing or the voices, and I couldn't stand hearing my dumbass voice over and over again, so I focused on shutting it up. She slid her hand up another inch. I moved my arm around her waist. She looked at me and smiled.

We stayed like that for some time. Probably an hour, but I'm not sure. The fire had died down to just a few glowing embers, and I could see the outline of Varsay trekking back towards the cabins with the other counselors. The "alone time" that he so generously granted us on Friday nights. I wanted to hug him, old Varsay, and thank him for his brilliance.

I turned to Jessica. She emanated warmth. I kissed her, and felt a smile on her lips. I loved that. It made me smile, too. I kissed her more, and tried to pull a mental picture of her pretty face, her deep brown eyes, her adorable laugh. I remembered her clothes, her walk, even the color of her sandals at the pool… but I couldn't remember her. It wasn't that I didn't want to, I just couldn't. My mind wouldn't allow it. The only girl I could picture was Julia Levin, standing there in front of me; hands jammed in her pockets with her shoulders slouched, giggling like she always does when I make her laugh, then grabbing my hand and pulling me off with her. She always knew when I wanted to do something but was too stubborn or proud to admit it, like dance with her when her favorite song came on, or sing to her, and she knew exactly how to coax it out of me. I'd pretend to be mad about it afterward, but I've secretly always loved it.

I couldn't for the life of me figure out why the hell I was thinking about Jules *right now*, and it was taking away from the moment, so I distracted myself by swinging my leg over the log bench to face Jessica. She was already a step ahead of me, and slid right into my lap as soon as I turned. I went up her shirt; she hadn't even *worn* a bra. I seriously gave up all hope of ever learning how to unhook one. Then her hand slid under my mesh shorts, grabbing me. I dug into her with my fingers and pulled her even closer, our breathing heavy. I dropped my hand down her lower back and under her shorts to squeeze her ass. She pushed herself onto me, letting out a quiet gasp, then a moan.

Then she stopped. She pulled back and looked me in the eyes, massaging me in her hands. She slid back on the bench and slowly lowered herself—never breaking eye contact—wrapping her wet lips around me. I tilted my head back, staring at the stars. She was an artist. Her tongue touched all the right places; she went slow, then fast and deep. It was exactly like the magazines had described.

"WHAT THE FUCK?!"

Varsay might as well have had a bullhorn and a fucking police siren. Jessica and I jumped so high out of our seats we nearly both landed the fire. She pulled her shirt back down just as fast as I jammed my dick back into my shorts. My mesh shorts.

Varsay and his goddamn flashlights, all forty of them. Like a cop ruining a great house party, he shined his light square into my retinas, then down at my crotch. I was now paralyzed *and* blind. I awkwardly tried to cover up, my hands over my nuts, but it was too late. He flicked the light over to Jessica, whose tracks were covered much better than mine, then clicked off his light.

"Mr. Clark. Looks like you've been having a good time this evening." I couldn't see him, but I could hear it in his voice that he was smiling ear to ear. "Why don't you lead the way?"

I took Jessica's hand, and started down the path.

"So sorry to interrupt boys and girls, but it's time to call it a night. Back to your bunks," he said.

Jessica and I couldn't stop smiling the whole way back. I put my arm around her as we walked. She put her hand down my pants again. I liked Jessica. A lot.

CHAPTER TWELVE

Kyle was born on February 29, 1988. Leap day on a leap year.

That year we celebrated his fifteenth birthday on the 28th of February. On the 1st of March, a letter came to the Hall house notifying the family that Kyle's mother had died. Emma intercepted it in the post before Mr. Hall got home, and broke the news to their family over dinner. Kyle called me afterwards, asking if I wanted to bike up to Rita's for some water ice.

Emma took it the hardest. As annoying as she may have been, she had a huge heart. With no one to turn to in a house full of men, she had idolized her absent mother. Mrs. Hall was the stolen saint of her life; the great heroine of her world who was taken from her for reasons unknown when she was too young to remember. Mr. Hall refused to talk about her, and Emma had learned early on not to talk back to her father, so the case of her disappeared mother went cold.

Emma was a scribbler. She was always jotting things down in a book or drawing pictures of leaves or rocks or beetles while Kyle and I practiced guitar. She would question us relentlessly. "What do you like to write songs about, Kyle?" and "If you could pick, what color would your perfect guitar be?" Kyle was always quick to tell her to shut up and go away, but she had surprisingly thick skin for her age. Some days I felt bad for her; she was just trying to join in on our conversation like all little sisters do. She looked up to her older brother; with Mr. Hall being the drunken wreck he was, Kyle was the defacto man of the house. She loved him, idolized him. All she wanted was some attention from *someone* in her family. Someone to tell her how beautiful her drawings were, or how intelligent and pretty she was. Instead, she ended up with a hateful brother and his asshole friend, and a lame, drunken excuse of a father.

Fortunately for her, Mr. Hall was hardly interested in Emma. Aside from supplying him the occasional human punching bag, she wasn't really his taste. It was Kyle he took a liking to.

Mr. Hall and his drunk, southern-accented self-decided it was time he taught his son how to be a man; taught him how to fight off the oppressor. "In life, most of the time yer opponent will be bigger 'n stronger than you; you have to learn how to adapt. Be cunning like the fox, and savvy like the Chinks. It's brains that win in the end, not muscle." He would say, stumbling to the kitchen for more whisky.

I never pressed on the issue because Kyle never wanted to talk about it. More than once he'd come over to my house in the morning with bruises around his neck, and he'd just want to sit around all day and do nothing. We would play video games, which he never liked, but on those days it was all he wanted to do. He didn't want a turn either; he just wanted to watch me play. We'd order pizza, or put on a Pink Floyd album and just zone out. Sometimes he would just knock out for a few hours.

I'd bring up his Dad occasionally, in an off-hand way, but he would always tell me to shut up and forget about it, so I did.

There was an old, beat up garage at the back end of Kyle's

driveway that we adopted as our hideout that year. The original pine tree fort had grown too small for us; after all, we were in high school now, it was time we made the switch. There was a boatload of power tools in the garage; hammers, drills, nails and screws, all waiting to be put to good use. Alongside the driveway were two trees with perfectly parallel trunks; the ideal location for our new tree house.

We biked down to the local hardware store some fifteen blocks down West Chester Pike to buy the lumber we needed. It only took about nine trips back and forth from the shop, balancing 8x2x4's and thick sheets of 5-ply plywood between the two of our bikes, riding straight down the middle of the road. Where there's a will, there's a way.

Our tree house was a "platform" design, a primitive but respected style among tree house builders, as far as we knew. We nailed up v-shaped supports, and slid pieces of plywood over in place to act as the base of our fort. There were two sections, the main big one and a small upper platform, similar to a ship's deck and a crow's nest. Our crow's nest was level with the third floor of the houses around us, a significant height increase from our previous hideouts. It should also be noted that it was perfectly eye level with Lindsey's bedroom window, and that this was not at all a coincidence. We painted it a sloppy green and brown camouflage to match the foliage and go unnoticed, letting it settle for a few days while the polyurethane dried. From that day on, it was our after-school spot.

We also built a loft section into the rafters in the garage. When it rained, we'd retreat there. We would listen to the storm for hours, droplets pelting off the garage roof just a few inches from where we sat. In Philly it's cold and rainy from November to May; we were in the garage a lot. We would talk about camp and the girls we had met, or brainstorm on how to get new ones, or talk about which chicks we thought were hottest at school. We had pretty similar taste, so it was fun to put together our *Top 10* lists, even if all ten of them were out of our league. You can't fault dreamers for dreaming.

It was on one of those rainy afternoons that Kyle presented to me our next business venture.

"Check this out," he said, handing me a small plastic sandwich baggie. I held it up close to my face, staring at two green nuggets with absolutely no idea what I was looking at.

"Weed," he said.

Weed. I had heard about it. The rebels of our high school class had done it and told stories, so of course I knew about "getting high." This was the first time I actually held weed in my hand, which gave me a strange sensation of power. I unzipped the bag and inhaled. It was the first time I had ever smelled that sticky, potent aroma that good weed has.

"Where did you get it?" I asked.

"Mitch from across the street. Sold it to me for forty-five bucks. It's an eighth," he told me. In reality it was closer to a dime piece, but how were we supposed to know?

"Do you know how much we can sell that for if we break it up into grams? Twenty bucks a pop," he said. You could see the excitement in his eyes.

I pondered. Extra cash on the side would really propel our music in the right direction. A legitimate, career-launching direction; we'd print *real* CD's, rent out a *real* recording studio, and finally become *real* artists. After all, the difference between a real artist and a fake one is only money, and no one cares about the starving ones. They starve because no one cares. It's no secret what you have to do, Kyle and I did it at camp two years in a row: create great product (*Run of the Mill* music), market it to your targeted demographic (the girls at camp), build up buzz (get the girls at camp excited and they get everyone else at camp excited), release the product (tapes, CDs), and promote it (live shows at camp)!

Imagine what we could do with thousands of dollars behind us…

We didn't care about the weed itself; neither of us had ever smoked it nor had any interest in smoking it. We were excited at the idea of starting a business and conquering the city. Monopolizing the market as partners in crime.

I was on board from the minute he handed me the baggie. "I'm in. Let's do it!" I said.

And thus, the Kyle-Tyler marijuana business was born.

We started buying in bulk from a senior named Chris Navarro. He had this white Bronco truck with a sick aftermarket stereo system installed that played videos of snowboarders and surfers while you listened to the radio. He also had a couple of neon lights that he could flick on to light up the whole truck. It was a genuine ricer. That's how we knew he was the real deal.

Kyle, being the ambitious salesman he was, had us buying in bulk from the start; three ounces at a time. For those of you who may not know how much weed an ounce is, just imagine filling up a typical sandwich bag with shredded lettuce until it's bulging out from the edges and difficult to zip closed. That's pretty much how much an ounce is. We bought a strain that was nicknamed "Durban Poison." All business was done in cash, and our purchase cost us around $250/oz.

There are about twenty-eight grams in an ounce, which we purchased for less than ten dollars per gram, and then turned around and sold for thirty dollars per gram. We usually flipped three ounces in a month:

$30/gram x 28 grams/oz. x 3oz - ($250/oz. x 3oz) = $1,770.00 profit per month.

In it to win it.

Aside from our dealer Chris, we were the only kids in our high school with the balls to sell pot, so everyone came to us. And I mean *everyone*. Freshman, sophomores, juniors, seniors, art kids, jocks, Goths, nerds, hippies, suck ups, you name it. Take a look at your Econ 101 supply and demand graph and it's easy to see why we were able to make such a killing. We controlled the market. Over $1,700 a month, purely profit.

But there was a negative side to it all. Addiction is something that starts slowly and then consumes you. Walking around with sometimes twenty grams of illegal drugs in your pocket and then selling it to your peers for 200% profit is an addicting thrill. I won't pretend like it's not. Defying the law, learning to maintain your cool and keep a straight face as you walk past police officers, jumping in and out of cars with hundreds of dollars bursting out of your pockets—more money than you could have ever imagined at fifteen—this is what gets you in trouble. A fifteen year old with that kind of money is always going to get into trouble.

Kyle got in trouble.

CHAPTER THIRTEEN

Power has an interesting effect on the ego. It can be dangerous, of course; history has shown us far too many times the millions of lives lost at the hands of corrupt leaders. However, in more rare cases, power can manifest positive results.

As the go-to connect for my entire school's weed needs, I garnered significant celebrity status for the first time ever. My peers treated me differently; upperclassmen respected me, underclassmen feared and loved me. I'm not kidding. Kids bought me lunches, gave me gifts like advanced copies of new PS2 games or remastered Led Zeppelin albums, and invited me to parties *every* weekend. It was a big deal for someone who normally spends his Saturday nights watching movies alone in his bedroom.

I had six or seven tables to choose from at lunch; a welcomed change from my usual spot in the back corner at the retard table. That's not an insult, or politically incorrect language. It was literally where the mentally disabled kids sat. Half of the table was silent because they physically couldn't speak, and the other half was a shouting match between upset autistic kids. I was friends with Allen Jenkins, one of the sweetest human beings

I've ever had the pleasure of knowing, whom, certainly not by choice, received an extra twenty-first chromosome. I would hang out with him every other week or so. We would play soccer out back, or play SOCOM on PS2, or trade Pokémon cards. Sometimes, when he was really, *really* happy, I would catch glimpses of him. It was his true inner self, trapped—wanting *so desperately* to get out. At least that's how it seemed to me. Maybe they were my own projections, just trying to make sense of it all, wishing I could get to know Allen's unabridged personality. Downs Syndrome is *hard* (understatement of the year). Allen's family lived a few houses down from mine, and on nights when Granddad had to work late, Grandmom and I would bake casseroles and walk down the block to have dinner with their family. We tried to help out as much as we could; Allen's his mother and father were overworked and underpaid, both professionally and in life. You could see how tired they were; it was in their eyes, in their wrinkles, in their voices; but they always found reason to smile. That's what I loved about them.

Really, I sat at the back table because Kyle had a different lunch period than I did, and I didn't have any other friends in 2nd lunch.

Everyone now liked me because of what I had to offer, not necessarily because of who I was. But that wasn't important. I was blossoming. Their constant compliments and high regards tore at my thick outer binding, and I clawed like hell from the insides. After a few months of fighting at it, I was free. The power I was given didn't turn me evil… it woke me up.

I graduated from the "oh, I didn't even realize you went to this school" clique to the "cool" and "edgy" ones. I was popular *and* a law-breaker, which shoveled me into the "bad-boy" genre. Badass.

Girls noticed me. Emma, this cute blonde girl I'd sat next to all year in American History, learned my name for what was definitely the first time in the ten years I'd known her. Rachel from sewing class partnered up with me every other day when we paired up to work on cross-stitching. Even Erika in my English class, inarguably the hottest girl in our grade, volunteered to work Shakespeare sides with me: Macbeth and Lady Macbeth. It was fitting, actually. She was mental.

The only one who didn't treat me differently was Jules. I hadn't talked to her in months. I hadn't hung out with her in years…and I missed her. She had new friends and lived a new lifestyle, as did I; which tore us apart up until the moment she walked into my pre-Calc class in January. The Gods were kind that day, and laid common ground so that neither of us had any real friends in that class, which reunited us.

I half expected her to be the same old Jules, digging worms with me in the compost pile, asking me if I would ever marry her or date her or be friends with her forever, and dragging me around the pool deck. And she was. She was the same dork I'd always known. I was the one who'd changed.

I was finally able to successfully vocalize my personality without completely embarrassing myself. It was everything Jules had always wanted to pry out of me, and I could tell she was thrilled that I'd finally come around. I could articulate my thoughts and actual reciprocate conversation. We instantly reconnected, which was great because about twenty minutes later we were partnered up to present parametric equations to our fellow pre-Calc classmates in a few weeks, which meant we'd be seeing a lot of each other, in continuum, very soon.

Kyle had his own prerogatives, and slipped in with the "stoner" crowd. I didn't exactly condone it, but I didn't want to make a big deal out of it either, so I gave it all a mild shrug and carried on. Something about the weed-head mentality didn't click with me. I found it empowering to better myself; gripping the negatives in my life by the horns and fighting them back; making our marijuana business more profitable, personally becoming more sociable and active in making friends, and living life were the challenges I embraced. Stoners sought to escape confrontation, conversation, and communication. I'm not a hater; it's just not for me.

Kyle was happy, and I was happy, and if it ain't broke, I don't fix it.

"The first section is on page forty-eight," Jules said, flipping through her textbook. I dropped my backpack on the table and collapsed on the couch. I was hungry. "Did you bring your textbook?" she asked. She had me pegged as a slacker because I hung out with Kyle so much, which is reasonable because he *was* a big slacker, but I actually did really well in school. I liked to learn, and I liked to excel when tested.

"Yeah, I brought it, relax," I said, hoping she wouldn't call my bluff. It was a seven hundred-page textbook that weighed like fifteen pounds. I didn't take it out of my locker unless I absolutely had to. "Do we have to start right this second?"

She closed her textbook and turned to me. "No," she said. I let out an exaggerated sigh of relief. Out of the corner of my eye, I saw her smile. "What do you propose we do?"

"Does your mom buy pizza bagels?" I asked.

"No. But she left me twenty dollars for dinner. Let's order pizza!"

She called up and ordered from Cenzos, and then plopped down on the couch next to me. She had the TV on mute, flipping through channels, searching for a movie.

"My mom bought me pizza bagels… once," she said.

"A momentous occasion."

"Those times may be gone, but never forgotten." She flipped through more channels. Horrible daytime TV and five o'clock news. "You know what's annoying, though? She never leaves a note anymore. She used to always leave a note," she said.

"What kind of note?" I asked.

"Any kind. Nothing fancy, just a sticky or something scribbled down on a napkin letting me know she'd be home late, or that she put dinner in the microwave, or had left me money."

"She still leaves you the money, so who cares?" I said. I had a knack for being tremendously blind to oncoming sentimental moments.

"Yeah, I guess. I just miss them," she said.

She retreated to the corner of the couch, a pillow bunched snugly in her arms, legs tucked in towards her chest. Her toes wiggled occasionally in their pink and white socks at the edge of the cushion. We simmered in the blue-ish glow of the screen for a few minutes.

"You need a release," I said. She looked at me, waiting for more. "Granddad always told me soccer was his release, and that it should be mine too." I said.

"You hate soccer," she giggled.

"It's a terrible release. It just pisses me off even more, all of those douches rambling on about their training diets, juggling tricks, FIFA 2004—"

"Be nice. They're not that bad."

"Who the hell plays FIFA?"

"Not everyone can be as cool and hipster as you, Ty," she said.

"You're more hipster than me."

"Oh, am I?"

"Look at your socks! And that pillow. And that scarf you wore the other day—"

"What! You said you liked my scarf—"

"And the TV shows you watch." Neither of us had been paying attention to the TV, and Jules had stopped flipping through about ten minutes ago, but "Antique Roadshow" was on now, and I had her pinned. We both laughed.

"I did like that scarf." I said.

"*You* need a release," she said.

"Music." It came out very matter of factly. For a moment it had me wondering why I didn't devote more time to the only thing I really knew, and loved, and trusted.

"Where did you learn to play?" Her voice was more somber now, and she had shifted her weight, opening up to me on the couch. I think she wanted to…*talk*.

"Kyle and I taught ourselves," I said. She rolled her eyes at the mention of his name.

"Did your parents play?"

It sounded almost like she immediately regretted asking, so I tried to play it off like it wasn't a sore spot. I didn't want her to feel bad. And honestly, it wasn't as bad as it used to be, when I was younger. I just didn't like talking about my parents because I hardly had anything to say. I didn't know them.

"No. Grandmom tells me stories sometimes about my dad and his records, how he nearly drove her mad because he used to play the same song all day--"

"*Ah!* I *knew* that had to be genetic!"

This time *I* rolled my eyes. "Fuck you," I said, sarcastically.

"You are the worst with that!"

"It's not that bad. When have you ever even heard me do it?"

"Um, hello, I live next door. You blast the same stupid song for hours straight. It's so loud it sounds like you're pointing your speakers out the window."

"What terrible songs do I play?" I asked.

"Hotel California."

"What!"

"Stairway to Heaven."

"What!?"

"...Wish You Were Here." She buckled over, laughing.

"You are an evil woman, you know th--"

"That song too! Oh God, you *never* stop playing that song!"

"That's because it's a frickin' great song," I said, pretending to be incredibly insulted. I crossed my arms and gave her an exasperated *"humph,"* which made her laugh even more. Her laugh always made me laugh.

"What kind of music did he like?" She asked after a few minutes of catching her breath. She scooted in closer to me, hanging her leg over mine.

"Led Zeppelin, Pink Floyd, Hendrix, The Beatles. The same stuff we like," I said. She gave me a perplexed look, tilting her head to the side like a puppy. "Well, the same bands *I* like," I said.

"I bet you're a lot like your dad... and your mom."

"A profoundly scientific statement."

"You know what I mean, loser," she said, smacking me on the shoulder. "I don't feel like doing this. Parametric equations are for pussies. Let's watch a movie," she said. She definitely hung around with me too much growing up. She was a bro.

She stood up and walked over to the bureau to pick out a DVD. She was wearing this ripped up baggy shirt that occasionally flashed her stomach and part of her bra, depending on the angle. She kind of half-tucked it into her sweatpants, which were rolled over a few times and barely hanging from her hips. With every step her butt bounced, pushing her hips side to side. It was fucking sexy.

I slapped myself, and buried my head into the pillow, mad for even thinking it. I'd known Jules my whole life. She knew me better than my own Grandparents. I watched her throw her hair over to one side and bend over slightly, scanning the shelf. She leaned in further to get a closer look. Super-close. I mean, it was seriously the distance only a legally blind person would need to be at. I was about to make fun of her, but then she kept bending lower, arching her back, ass out, scanning intently for the perfect film. There were only about fifteen movies on the shelf, it really shouldn't have ever taken this long, but she continued to browse, sliding her fingers across the spines of the cases one by one, slowly rolling her hips around as she shifted her weight from one leg to the other.

"Yes!" She said, whipping around to me, brandishing *Gangs of New York*. I smiled and nodded, wiping the drool.

Our parametric equations presentation sufficed a B+, which was actually like an A because our teacher was a total dick and never gave out A's because he felt tough stealing the joy and pride away from sixteen year olds. But we were pumped. We celebrated with water ice, and went out to eat with the money her mom left her. I was feeling particularly rebellious and tried to get served, a glass of wine for dessert, which got us laughed out of the restaurant. It totally would have worked, but Jules couldn't keep a straight face.

We spent more and more time together, like when we were younger, except not the same. I didn't have any more sexual moments around her like the time with the DVD, mostly because when we hung out we were always fully clothed and it was winter, so I wrote that day off as a one-timer, never to be worried about. I mean, who wouldn't be attracted to a girl sensually writhing around in low-cut sweatpants and a nearly see-through shirt?

That's not to say things weren't more charged than usual. I felt connected to her, like she was a part of me; someone I could completely trust my secrets, my sorrows, and my soul with. I was comfortable around her. We joked about everything, talked trash on everyone, and best of all, we genuinely enjoyed each other's company. To the point where I would head over to her place every day and stay until eleven or twelve at night. My grandparents weren't thrilled with my requested curfew deadline extension, but they were happy to see me hanging out with someone other than Kyle.

The marijuana business continued to grow. Operations were routine and low-stress. Kyle and I were crushing the market; outdoing *and* underpricing the competition's product. I set up a few "bank accounts" for the two of us, so that we could keep track of the profits and organize our cash. I use quotations when I say "bank accounts," because these "bank accounts" were just shoeboxes jammed full of cash. I'd heard enough horror stories of the IRA raiding weed sellers' houses after zeroing in on their bank accounts, deposits, and spending habits, and fuck if I was going to open a bank account under my name to start dumping thousands of dollars in every few weeks, all cash. Kind of a red flag. I kept an accounting ledger, which I stashed under my nightstand in my room.

Our main conjoined savings account was for the next *Run of the Mill* album. I wanted to rent out a real studio, as opposed to engineering it myself. I thought it was time to step things up a notch, and finally, we had the means. It was going to be a chart-topping masterpiece for the motherfucking ages. I talked to Kyle about it every time I saw him, which was becoming less and less often. I prioritized my time and spent almost all of it with Jules now. Kyle and I didn't jam like we used to on the porch, and wrestling season was over, and the business was virtually hands-off at this stage. We didn't have much need to see each other anymore.

Then Kyle started getting high. Every day. It started as an

experiment, one that I never partook in, and evolved into a strange sort of addiction. Less an "addiction" and more a coping method. Kyle had become even more reclusive about his personal life. Something inside him had changed. He never wanted to hang out at his house anymore, or jam on his front porch like we used to. He just wanted to get as far away from his home as he possibly could.

All of a sudden, everything started to deteriorate between us; so fast it felt unreal. Kyle became spastically obnoxious and boisterous at school, like he was overcome by some PMS mood-swing disease. One minute he'd be happily laughing, working on a group project or something; the next, ripping apart textbooks and lighting homework assignments on fire in the back of the classroom. Some kids thought it was hilarious, entertained by the train-wreck of a spectacle he was becoming, but most got tired of it after his second or third stint. I was mad the first time I saw it; he was transforming into an attention-seeking asshole.

Teachers despised him, and he spent most of his days in the principal's office. It was bizarre to me because I could so easily tell when he was himself. When he was acting like a desperate jerk, it was just because he was looking for some sort of reaction, some glimpse of recognition or attention, like a fiend. It reminded me of the Crate incident in the wrestling room, when that black cloud of hate suddenly appeared, hovering over Kyle's every step, dictating his judgment. That wasn't Kyle. That was something else.

I didn't know what to do about it. Our *brothers in arms* connection slowly began to unravel, and a growing animosity crept its way in.

That summer we didn't hang out every day like we used to. We didn't hang out much at all. If we saw each other even a few times in a week it seemed a special occasion, and then became awkward. I was mad at him for constantly being high for no fucking reason, and he was pissed with me for making such a big goddamn deal out of it. Fights like that, when each person is fighting over something different, are rarely reconcilable. In just a few weeks our friendship was almost gone.

It killed me on the inside, but there was no way I was going to go apologize for something I wasn't even wrong about, so I waited him out. I'm guessing he was doing the same, because for two weeks we didn't speak.

Then camp arrived.

Both of us silently agreed to put our feelings aside for the sake of the great time we were guaranteed to have. Our standoff ceased, and we went back to being friends again.

CHAPTER FOURTEEN

I first saw her in the dusty parking lot at camp through the dirty windows of the car as we pulled in; our ancient Ford Taurus wagon puttering to a loud, embarrassing stop. Grandmom and Granddad took pictures like I *hadn't* been there for two straight years already, which lasted all of ten seconds before I stormed off.

Maybe it was the difference in the atmosphere; the trees, the sun, the bugs, the dirt. Maybe it was seeing her out of context; void of prejudice and completely naked. Maybe I'll never know, but she put me down for the count. She had a purple sleeping bag clutched to her chest. Her hair was up in a ponytail and bobbed as she walked. She had on short shorts with a pink Abercrombie & Fitch shirt on, and a V-neck revealing a thin gold necklace. Her eyes, the darkest brown I'd ever seen, were more piercing and beautiful than I'd ever remembered. I was overloaded with excitement and nerves. Julia Levin was at Camp Innabah.

"Jules!"

"Tyler! Hey," she said.

"What are you doing here?"

"I wanted to surprise you."

"I couldn't believe it was you when we pulled up," I said. I was shocked. This was great.

"Well, you talk about this place like it's the Holy Grail, and my mom would rather I be here than home alone all summer, so I asked her if I could come."

"You're going to love it here," I said.

"You think?" She looked around, taking it all in.

"Come on, I'll show you everything. Did you sign in yet?"

It was a hot week that year, so the counselors bumped up the pool days. I was thrilled and terrified every time I met up with her. My stomach was churning like mad on the walk down to the pool. It's not like I hadn't done it a million times before—literally, at Towertop pool, *every* summer for like seven straight years—but still, I was nervous. I'd tossed and turned the whole night, anxious for daylight to come so I could see her again. Now, here she was, all wet in her bathing suit looking directly at me, her head slightly cocked to the left, perplexed.

"Huh? What?" I asked, snapping back to reality. I had been staring at her for too long. She laughed.

"What kind of music do you guys play on the new album?"

"Oh, yeah. It's kind of like Nirvana's *Unplugged* album," I said.

"Who are Nirvana Unplugged again?"

I nearly choked on the pool water. "It's just Nirvana. They're a band, remember? I told you this like a million times. Kurt Cobain," I said, scowling. I explained to her this shit like two weeks ago at my house. I even played the album.

She smirked. "I'm just kidding. I remember." She splashed water in my face and dipped underwater.

"The album is an acoustic album, that's why it's called Unplugged," I said, rambling on as soon as she came back up.

"Oh, really?" She teased. "Who would've thought?"

"Uh, not you a few weeks ago."

"Burn! That's harsh, Ty. Don't be mean." She dipped her hair back in the water.

"I'll get you a copy," I said.

"Ok, awesome. They sound cool. And I want you, too."

I was staring again. I couldn't help it. There was something different about her.

"Your music, I mean. And the Nirvana guy too, but I mostly want to hear yours," she said with a wink.

I promised her I'd get her one of our CDs. *Run of the Mill* had upgraded to the compact disk that year. She flashed me this incredible smile, then dipped underwater again and swam to the other edge of the pool to regroup with her newfound girlfriends. They all looked at me, covering their mouths, trying to hide their giggling. I puffed my chest out, pushed my shoulders back, and proudly got out of the pool.

From then on, everything I did, I did carefully and with intent. I planned, and then second guessed. I sabotaged my own missions. Stupid things, little things; I made lunch awkward because I wouldn't stop mumbling and I was terrified of silence. I tried corny jokes and overly ambitious sarcastic remarks. I wanted to make her laugh, see her smile, sit with her, *talk*. It was awful and amazing, emasculating and empowering. As the week progressed I drew things out to savor every minute I spent around her. I caught myself staring into her eyes, and sometimes she'd catch me, and in my braver moments sometimes I wouldn't even look away. It was our little lustrous connection, that magnetic attraction, that sexual tension you want to keep building and intensifying until neither of you can hold off for a minute more. Every time I saw her I wanted to walk right up to her and grab her and kiss her.

It wasn't because I bitched out that I didn't make a move, it was because I didn't feel like it needed to be rushed. I'd been friends with Jules forever. I didn't want to ruin that. Sure, I wanted to pressure wash the quiver bone, battle dip the cranny axe, or cannon ball the fiddle cove. Jules was *hot.* But I wanted to be *in love* with her so much more, which changed my approach. I was falling in love, hard and fast, with Julia Levin.

Kyle made friendly with a strange looking girl named Kelsey that summer. I say "strange" because Kyle usually had great taste and high standards, but for whatever reason, this year he dropped them all. She was a bit… rough. She came to camp with her twin brother, Dom, who guarded her like a pit bull, which was entirely unnecessary. Needless to say, Kyle didn't have much luck with Kelsey. He third-wheeled it with me and Jules for most of the week.

Camp wasn't fun in the ways it usually was that year because Kyle was so obsessed with finding ways to sneak off and get stoned. He couldn't go an hour without bringing it up. Instead of talking about girls or music, he wanted to talk about weed strains and different types of highs, to the point where I was honestly embarrassed *for* him. He thought it was the coolest thing, to talk about drugs every two seconds.

"Ty, let's go out back and smoke," he was always asking, pressuring me, waiting for me to finally crack. I said no every time. He had Jules curious though, and eventually he broke her.

"Come on, Jules, come try it. You'll love it, I promise." he said, with his big fucking salesman smile. She didn't stand a chance.

"Well…ok. Maybe just this once," she said.

I was so pissed off watching them slink off together like crack fiends with their crack rocks, but there was nothing I could do. Kyle was his own man, and Jules could make her own decisions. I decided I'd make the best impression on Jules if I pretended like I was open to it and didn't mind, not to mention she knew about our business and it might seem weird that I was so pro-selling when I hated smoking, so I let them have their afternoon together. I went to the pool, hit the arts and crafts junction before dinner, and hung out with Dom and Kelsey for the night. They were surprisingly pretty cool. After I made it crystal clear to Dom I didn't want to fuck his sister he relaxed a little, and we managed to have some fun. They were extremely "Jersey," if you know what I mean by that, but I couldn't fault them. It was institutionalized in them to be orange. Besides, they were great company. Dom was a moron, which made for a pretty hilarious campfire sing-along. They took my mind off of Jules and Kyle.

That was the first time I knew I could no longer trust my best friend. I saw it in the way he looked at Jules. Like Golem fantasizing about his precious ring.

The next afternoon, the counselors caught Kyle behind the bathrooms, sucking down nugs of weed through his homemade tinny pipe; baggie of weed in hand. I guess he was at the point where he no longer cared enough to hide it.

A big part of me was pleased when I heard he'd been caught. I was hoping the slap on the wrist might be enough to snap him out of his obsession. But that son of a bitch talked his way out of everything. He smoked up the two counselors that caught him, and soon enough word spread to all of the counselors that Kyle had great weed, so for the rest of the week the whole lot of them would get high every night around the campfire after everyone else was sent to bed. He even got a handy from Lisa, the only hot counselor to grace the campgrounds in all three fucking years we attended.

It wasn't even impressive. If he'd focused his energy on something useful, like expanding the business, or *Run of the Mill,* then maybe. Wasting your talents to spend every minute of the day blazed? Anyone can do that. Fuck mediocrity.

CHAPTER FIFTEEN

Jules spent the rest of that summer in Bellgrove, PA, which was a small country town about an hour north of where we lived in Philly, because her parents were "on business" in Switzerland for two and a half months, whatever that meant. My grandparents were willing to drive me up once or twice to see her; but they grew tired of the long haul fast, and quickly dropped not-so-subtle hints that they weren't going to take me anymore. Unfortunately, I still had seven or eight months before I could apply for my driver's permit, so I was stuck.

But the odds shifted in my favor. I found out that Kyle's grandfather lived in Bellgrove, too, and after a quick *Yahoo! Maps* search I discovered his farmhouse was only three blocks away from Jules'. *Three blocks!* Of course, three blocks in Bellgrove isn't the same as three blocks in Philadelphia; her house was actually about four miles from Kyle's grandfather's house, but that wasn't important right now. I'd figure out a way to get there. I could walk, or bring a bike, or skateboard over. Not important. The fact that Kyle had a connection in the same *town*, let alone the same neighborhood as Jules, was unbelievable.

What was important now, was figuring out how the hell I was going to convince Kyle that we should visit his grandfather once or twice a week, so that I could see Jules once or twice a week. My motivation wasn't exactly a secret though,, and given how rocky things already were between Kyle and me, I needed to provide him an incentive. It was time for *me* to don the salesman suit, and figure out how to convince Kyle that going to Bellgrove was a phenomenal idea.

"Have you ever thought about cutting out the middle man?" I asked. Kyle was up in the crow's nest with his binoculars, trying to catch a glimpse of Lindsey. She wasn't home, she went to Volleyball practice on Tuesdays and Thursdays, but he refused to believe me.

"What do you mean?"

"Well, we're constantly paying top rate for our weed when I think we could get it for cheaper."

"How?"

I didn't say anything back; I wanted to give time for the initial thought to seep in. He dropped his binoculars and climbed down to the main platform where I sat, playing SNAKE on my Nokia.

"I've been thinking about it a lot, so I did some research. Chris gives us a pretty good deal, but I'm sure if we asked around we could find a supplier closer to the source." I said.

"Wholesale?" he asked. I nodded, paused, and then shook my head.

"Sure, we could do that… but what if we didn't have to buy it at all…" I let it hang in the air. Kyle was smoking half of our stash these days and the business was slowly falling apart; we were hardly making any money, and in order to patch things up we'd either have to raise our prices or convince him to stop smoking it all, neither of which I was interested in doing. It was more trouble than it was worth. The only reason I'd kept it alive was to see Jules. "What if we grew it ourselves?" I said.

I saw the light bulb go off.

"Holy shit! That's the best idea I've ever heard!" He nearly squealed, and almost tripped over the edge of the platform. He was high out of his mind again. "It would be pure, 100% profit!"

"We just have to find a spot to grow it," I said. He stewed for a moment.

"What about *The Grange*? There's that wooded area in the back that could work." He said.

I shook my head and let my eyes drift around as though I were deep in thought. I already knew where the conversation was heading, but I had to make sure this came across like it was a spur-of-the-moment brainstorming session. I should've been an actor. Kyle was also really easy to predict when he was stoned. "There are too many dirt bikers back there, they'd find it and steal it," I said.

"Huh." he said. "Yeah, you're probably right."

"We need a big, open space, so we can grow a lot, but in an area that will go undetected."

"We live in Philly Ty, where the hell are we gonna find a spot like that?"

"We won't find it here, you're right." I let out a long sigh of defeat.

"We need a farm," he said.

"Yeah…"

He was picking at a small piece of splintered wood on the platform, and I wasn't sure if he was thinking, or just ADHD.

"Bellgrove," he said, softly at first. Then, "Bellgrove!"

Yessss, yes my child. Let your impotence be exorcised! Bellgrove…

"My grandfather lives up in this town called Bellgrove, and has acres of land there; we could grow right in the back of his cornfield!"

There it was. All his idea. Inception.

"You don't think he'd notice?" I asked.

"I don't think he'd care even if he did," he said.

"Perfect..."

"We'll have to go up there a lot, though. Like maybe twice a week, especially in the beginning. To make sure everything is growing right."

I didn't want to look too eager, and was trying my damnedest to hide my smile. "We're going to make some crazy money," I said. "I'm in if you are."

"I'll go call my grandpop now," he said, jumping down from the platform.

I watched him run inside. I was on cloud nine. This was going to be perfect.

My transportation issues were solved; one of the SEPTA railways went from a neighboring town called Hardmore to Bellgrove for five bucks. The station was a thirty-minute bike ride from our houses, which was a distance we were more than willing to travel in pursuit of our illicit botany experiment. Kyle bought the seeds from our dealer Chris, who was too stupid to realize he was digging his own grave, and we hit the road.

There was a massive weeping willow tree off the left side of Kyle's grandfather's property that we became completely infatuated with. Year after year our tree house plans had grown more complex, and this year we were set on creating a legitimate house; four walls and a roof, a retractable rope ladder, and an outer deck extension.

After showing him our blueprints, Kyle's grandfather had no problem with us building onto the tree. He even offered to help pay for the lumber, which we happily accepted.

Within three weeks of our start date, we had fully built our new hideout. *Run of the Mill Headquarters*.

"This way no one can get up who doesn't need to be here," Kyle explained, pulling up the ladder. It was exciting even if there wasn't much point to it; no one other than the two of us, save Kyle's grandfather, would ever even see the tree house, let alone give a shit enough to bother climbing up.

We planted our Cherry Bush marijuana seeds about sixty yards east of the base of the tree; so that we could keep guard and monitor growth from the deck above. They had already sprouted.

A few times that summer, Emma tagged along just to ruin our weekend. She was fourteen, and had big dreams to become a novelist. As if she wasn't annoying enough, now she had an excuse to ask a million and one questions about stupid stuff no one cared about, so that she could write it down in her journals. When Emma was around, that rope ladder was worth twice its weight in gold.

"Why did you build the tree house all the way out here, instead of in our backyard at home?"

"Because we felt like it." Kyle said.

"Why do you take the train to Grandpop's house all the time just to hang out in a tree house?"

"Because we want to."

"Are you even going to paint it?" She asked.

"Probably."

"All houses get painted. You have to paint the tree house."

Kyle was high out of his mind, so he didn't much mind Emma's interrogation.

Other times she would find herself in the wrong place at the wrong time; Kyle would be in an extremely bad mood and curse her out, or throw her out.

"Kyle, why don't you have a girlfriend?" she asked on

afternoon, standing on the HQ deck. I'd convinced Kyle to let her up to check out our handiwork.

Kyle turned bright red, and then went dark. It was that darkness from before; something he'd become all too comfortable with in the past year. A storm was coming.

"Why do you eat so much? You fat shit," he said, and then kicked her off of the main deck. Literally, he booted her in the back, right between the shoulder blades, and laughed as she flipped over the railing and plummeted some thirteen feet to the ground. She broke her arm and two ribs when she landed in the dirt below. Kyle thought it was hilarious, buckled over on the deck in hysteria. I was horrified watching Emma crawl into the house as her lip and nose gushed blood. She clutched her broken arm, and cried for her grandfather. She was a sweet girl, so innocent and curious, just trying to get know her big brother. Lord knows her father wasn't going to love her. My heart hurt for her.

CHAPTER SIXTEEN

I didn't tell Kyle about Jules' convenient location until we were in his grandfather's cornfield, trotting down the rows towards the way back of the property. I pretended my phone went off, looking at a text message.

"Oh shit, dude! Jules' house is only a couple blocks from here, she says." On second thought, I would be the worst actor. I felt my face cringe, and then tried to hide it, which only made it more obvious. I stared at my phone. I could feel his skepticism.

"Really…"

"Yeah, like a couple blocks. I told her we were coming up here today," I muttered.

"Really?"

"Yeah… really."

"Wow…" he said, peeling a stalk of corn. It must have been the most interesting piece of corn in the world because he stared at it for a full minute. Seriously, an entire sixty seconds ticked off. Then he snapped back to life. "Awesome! Let's go say what's up!"

Maybe there *was* a good side to Kyle constantly being high.

I rang the doorbell. I hadn't seen Jules in a few weeks, and my mind was running wild again. What if she didn't like me anymore? Met someone else? *Kissed* someone else? What if she wanted Kyle instead of me? I looked over at Kyle, who was playing with the berries on the bush by the mailbox. Nah, not likely. He regressed into a six year old when he smoked.

Her grandmother answered. She was a plump woman with short graying hair, a big smile, and an even bigger heart. She welcomed us like we were family; whipped up a homemade Chex-mix bowl (which Kyle devoured), and asked us those questions all grand moms ask about school, family, the weather, and our hobbies, while we waited for Jules to finish getting dressed. I like to think I handled the interview pretty well.

When Jules walked into the kitchen, I nearly lost it. She had on skinny jeans and tank top, her curly brown hair falling just below her shoulders. With a cute smile she stopped and shrugged at the two of us, her hands jammed in her pockets, waiting for our reaction.

Kyle launched forward and gave her an audacious hug, which snapped me out of my stupefied trance. He knew I liked her, I don't know why he was always going at her so hard. I followed suit and hugged her too. She smelled like spring flowers, like lilacs, or roses, or whichever flowers smell the best. Holding her felt so right; like I belonged there, in her arms—warm, gentle. I didn't want to let her go. I never wanted to let her go.

"How are you guys!"

"Great!" Kyle blurted out; way too loud for the tiny space we were in. He was swaying, his eyes webbed with bright red veins from the blunt he inhaled on the walk over.

"You look great," I said meekly. I didn't want her grandmom to hear. Jules tried to suppress her smile.

"Thank you," she whispered. "Let's go downstairs, I'll show you the basement!"

We hung out in her basement that afternoon, watching movies. Seating arrangements were split between the couch and the single chair. Jules and I took the couch, Kyle took the chair.

The mood was light and filled with energy. The initial awkwardness evaporated as soon as we sat down, and we all started reminiscing on good times at camp. The spark between Jules and I was developing into a flame. She would touch my arm and hold on to it for a few minutes, or I would grab her hand and nudge closer to her. I think we both wanted to see what might happen.

Kyle went to the bathroom, finally giving us a moment alone.

"Tyler," she said.

"Hey."

"Kiss me."

I had been waiting for her to say that for months. Probably even years. Probably since the day I met her, I just hadn't realized it. My heart skipped a beat. I pulled her in and touched her lips to mine.

Then Kyle burst out of the bathroom.

"Let's smoke!" he damn near screamed, collapsing back on the chair. I wasn't sure if he'd seen us kiss. Even if he did, I doubt he would have remembered it.

I'm terrible at hiding when I'm in a bad mood, and this really pissed me off. I fucking hated when he did this, this weed smoking bullshit every two seconds. He brought it up every chance he could, *especially* when Jules was around. It was obviously a jealousy thing; he didn't like being left out of the mix. I let out a long, loud sigh, rolled my eyes, and flicked the TV remote. Not much I could do at this point.

"Um, I'm ok, actually," Jules said.

"Really?" Kyle asked. He sounded just as shocked as I was. "I've got some crazy weed! You'll love it, Jules."

"Thanks, but I'm ok right now." She smiled and turned back towards the TV.

"Just smell this nugget," he said, jamming the bag of weed in her face. She pushed it away.

I knew Kyle, and I knew his intentions, and I knew his goddamn addiction to smoking weed, and I *hated* every part of it all. When Jules declined his offer, I felt my whole body flutter with warmth. I was… proud of her. This was Kyle's best move and it had *failed*. Kyle never fails. *Kyle gets what he wants.*

"She said no, dude."

"Huh?" he said, trying to ignore me.

"She said no." I said, louder.

"Alright, chill out Ty."

"I will once you back off. She doesn't want to fuckin' smoke with you. Go smoke by yourself."

"I don't know what your problem is, dude. You hate weed for no reason."

"I don't give a shit about the weed. What I hate is that you act like a fuckin' heroin addict with it. You can't go twenty minutes without sucking down a bowl."

"You can't even get addicted to pot, dumbass."

"That's not the point."

"What is?"

"Tyler, really, it's ok," Jules cut in.

"All you do is talk shit behind my back, Ty. If you think I don't know about it, you're retarded." Kyle said. "If she wants to smoke, she can smoke. You can't control her."

"She just *told you* ten times she doesn't want to. She doesn't want to smell the fuckin' nugget either, dude. Just go out back by yourself."

Jules jumped up and skipped over to the back door, attempting to dissipate some of the tension. "Here, Kyle. You can go out right through this door. No one will see you out there." She opened it for him.

"Go on." I said.

"I will."

Kyle went out back alone to smoke his tree and I stayed inside with Jules who, as soon as the back door shut, was on top of me. She locked the door and threw herself onto me, pressing me against the couch armrest, grinding on me in a pulsing motion, passionate, melodic. I pressed back, grinding with her in a sexual rhythm we were both discovering for the first time. I wanted her so bad—every inch of her. I ripped her shirt off and unhooked her bra (finally confirming I know how to take off a girl's bra—hell yeah) while she tore my belt off and wrestled with my jeans.

For weeks... *months*... we had waited for this.

"Tyler," she whispered.

I slipped the top button of her jeans open. She kissed me harder, so I continued. With two hands I pulled her jeans down over her ass. She let out a gasp as I grabbed it and squeezed. God, it was perfect. I slid my fingers underneath.

"Do it," she moaned.

I kept kissing her neck, sliding my fingers inside of her. I wanted to turn her world upside down. I didn't know much, but I definitely knew I was doing *something* right, because she let out a soft, low moan, then slipped her hand under my belt and grabbed me.

"Fuck me," she whispered. "I want you to fuck me."

I paused and looked at her. She was so beautiful, locked in with me, sexy as hell. I shot a glance at the back door; I could see Kyle's tiny figure slowly disappear into the woods at the edge of the backyard. He'd be gone for a while.

I lifted her up and flipped her over onto her back, gently, so that the back of her head rested on the pillow by the arm of the sofa. She grabbed around my neck with both hands and kissed me fiercely as I slid into her. *Oh my god.* My mind was blown. *This* is what it feels like.

Sex… *sex is power.* It was more powerful than anything I'd ever experienced. I was in love and I knew it.

She came. I could feel it, and she dug her fingernails into my back and screamed. I put my hand over her mouth to try to muffle it, her grandmom was still home, but in the moment neither of us cared. She laughed, pulling my hand off of her mouth.

"You trying to shut me up?"

"You were making too much noise," I said, laughing. She kissed me again.

"That was incredible…"

"We're just getting started…" I said, slowly pushing back in with confidence.

About thirty seconds later, it was done.

She went to pee while I unlocked the back door to check for Kyle. He was lying in the middle of the yard, arms and legs outstretched like a snow angel, sleeping. I left him there and went back inside to Jules.

After that first time, we fucked everywhere. Sex was *fun*. We had grown so comfortable with each other, and we were so in love. We experimented, we teased, we created games. You name a public space, we did it. Parking lots, museums, movie theaters, while driving, at friends' houses, the woods, the backyard, the kitchen, dining room, bedroom, and of course the basement. All day. All night. I started a boy, and finished a man.

As weeks progressed, Kyle and I continued to make trips up to Bellgrove for the sake of our business, but it was obvious that I only went to see Jules. He knew it, and I knew it pissed him off.

One afternoon while he was blazing up on the side of the house, I went through his backpack. I know I shouldn't have, but I did. He had a notebook with some drawings in it and a few pictures of him and Jules from camp. It was harmless, but as I continued to flip through the book, the drawings got more intense. Drawings of the two of them together all over the world; Paris, Mexico, Canada. Drawings of the two of them at the alter, reading their vows. Drawings of them copulating.

It freaked me out.

I needed to find him a girl.

In the meantime, I tried to distract him with the weed we were growing. I made sure the marijuana crops stayed healthy, and after a few months they started to flower. We sold about half of the stock, but the business was no longer a priority for either of us. Still, my focus was keeping Kyle happy and occupied so that I could sneak off and meet up with Jules, so I encouraged him to smoke as much weed as his heart desired. He did.

I had also been working on my grandparents for *months*, trying to convince them into being comfortable with the idea of me sleeping over at Kyle's grandfather's farmhouse. I told them Kyle and I were working on a biology project, studying the growth cycle of corn stalks. We had to make sure we were there to collect data late at night and early in the morning, so it was necessary for me to stay the night. I had to put in a lot of effort to make the lie seem believable. I drew up lesson plans, homework assignments, project handouts, deadlines, and fake progress reports. By the time they agreed to let me stay, I was a goddamn expert on the genetic and biological makeup of a fucking piece of corn. Totally worth it.

We told Kyle's grandfather we were staying at our friend's house down the street, and that my grandparents were one hundred percent ok with it. Kyle's grandpop didn't ask questions, probably because he was slowly succumbing to Alzheimer's and most of the time didn't remember we were even in the house.

When we all hung out in Bellgrove, I made sure Jules invited a friend over for Kyle, but time after time that plan failed. Admittedly, a lot of Jules's friends weren't very attractive, but the problem lied with Kyle, not any of them. He didn't put in an ounce of effort; most of the time his small talk was either rambling on about some weed strain he'd found online, or making fun of something the girl said, or the music she liked, or the clothes she was wearing. He was a jerk.

We went to Bellgrove high school parties on the weekends. Jules worked as a lifeguard at the local pool and quickly made friends with Bellgrove kids our age. She was always great at that. Everywhere she went, people loved her. Jules and I figured there was a good chance Kyle would meet a fellow stoner chick and hit it off with her at a party, or at least find a girl drunk enough to sleep with him. We were running low on good ideas. Not to mention, we always had a great time at Bellgrove parties, so it was a win-win situation.

The first weekend I slept over was the weekend Jules' friend Kelly threw a house party. Her father was a partner at some big law firm, so their family was rich as hell, and her parents were always out of town on business trips. The house was a Victorian mansion with a pool and a hot tub in the backyard. The cabinets and fridge were stocked with beer, liquor, wine coolers, and 40 oz.'s. A few guys brought over a keg of Natty Light, and there was weed in the air all night. We arrived around 10:30 p.m., right as things were starting to get good. A group of bros were huddled around two slutty chicks fooling around in the hot tub, the football guys were playing water polo in the pool shirtless with the cheerleaders in their bikinis, and there was a huge dance party in the living room. It was perfect.

After a few drinks Jules and I were off to our usual escapade.

"Tyler, I have to show you something," she said, curling her index finger, leading me in to the master bedroom. I chugged the rest of my beer, tossed the can into the nearby umbrella stand, and followed her in. She was lying on her back on the bed with her legs in the air. I shut the door, clicked the lock. She pulled me in and unbuckled my belt.

Around 1:00 a.m. we found Kyle downstairs hanging out with a group of stoners, all dudes, listening to Pink Floyd's *Dark Side of the Moon*. He was pissed to have to leave, but the party was pretty much over and Jules and I were both ready to go to sleep.

When we slept over Jules' place we crashed in her basement; I bunked on the couch and Kyle squeezed into the Lay-Z-boy. I'm not sure why he didn't opt to sleep at his grandfather's house. That's what I would have done. But in fairness, we were all drunk and Kyle was high. I'm sure he didn't feel like walking four miles back to his Grandpop's house any more than I did.

Jules set her alarm to 4:00 a.m. and snuck down while everyone in the house snored away, including Kyle.

"Are you awake?" she whispered, shaking my shoulder lightly.

"Hey, yeah." I said, groggily. She was straddling me in nothing but a pair of sweatpants and a skimpy tank top.

"Good," she said, kissing me. Within seconds she was in my pants. She hovered over me, pulled her gray sweatpants down below her hips, and slid onto me. Tight, wet. We started slow, gently pulsing in and out in rhythm. She would balance herself with her left hand pressed on the center of my chest, her right arm up in the air, tilting her head back, letting out long, soft moans. Faster, and faster… the couch started to squeak. Her breath was hot on my neck. Her soft moans soon turned to muffled screams as she rode. She pressed her face into the pillow, convulsing, digging her nails into my back.

And then I saw him staring at me. His eyes black as the night.

I stopped moving. Jules was out of breath, still in the moment. "Why'd you stop!" she whispered loudly, smacking my chest. Her smile faded at my terrified look.

I pulled her close and whispered in her ear as quietly as I could, trying not to move. "He's watching us." She stopped. Completely still.

"He's *awake?*"

"Yes." I didn't want to look back. His black eyes were like staring into death itself. It was fucking terrifying. *Why was he staring like that?* Any normal person would have just turned around, or coughed loudly as a signal for us to knock it off.

We laid there motionless for probably thirty minutes, until we heard him snoring again. Jules leaped off and ran back up to her room. I pulled the covers back up and tried to get some sleep.

The next morning everyone acted like nothing had happened. But I never forgot. I never forgot those black eyes.

CHAPTER SEVENTEEN

It was summer in Philly, which is inarguably the best time of the year. The grass was green, the trees were full, the air was warm, and the girls were looking as sexy as ever. The weather in Philly is pleasant about three months out of the year so when it arrives, everyone pulls out the stops. Backyard barbecues every night, beers on the stoop with friends and neighbors, picnics and pick-up basketball in Fairmount Park, fresh lemonade and cheesesteaks down at Rittenhouse Square. On Fridays at 5:00 p.m., a small string quartet would perform for an hour in front of the fountain at Rittenhouse. I always loved that.

We caught the 5:47 p.m. train from Hardmore to Bellgrove. My stomach lurched in anticipation as we bumped along the rail line, stop by stop. Tonight was going to be one of the biggest parties of the summer in Bellgrove; Greg Seefeldt was hosting at his mom's house. They lived in a tiny apartment complex off of Ellis Woods Road, on the second floor. Seefeldt was notorious for throwing sick parties. Last winter, two idiots thought they could jump from his balcony to the neighboring one; they went for it, and ended up in the hospital. Broke three arms and an ankle combined. From then on, Seefeldt's mom's house was legendary.

"Psst. Kyle."

"What's up?"

"Grab one," I said, passing him one of the five 40oz Colt 45's I'd stashed in my guitar-less guitar case. We were still able to have a good time on summer nights like tonight, despite all that had happened. We cracked them open and clinked. "Bottom's up."

After a hearty dinner with Kyle's grandfather—chuck roast with green beans and angel food cake for dessert—Kyle and I cut through the cornfield out back over to Jules' house. She answered the door in a tight black dress and ushered us in to sit on the living room couches.

"I'll be ready in five minutes, be right back!" she said, scampering off. Naturally, those five minutes turned into forty, so Kyle and I uncapped our second Colt.

"How you feeling about tonight?" I asked. "Should be some cuties at this party."

"Yeah…"

"Jules was talking to a couple junior girls, hyping them up about you."

"I told you, you guys don't need to do that," he said.

"She's just priming them up. I checked them out in her yearbook… they're both pretty hot."

"Don't bullshit me."

"I'm not! I'd fuck 'em," I said.

"Saying that doesn't help your case," he said, grinning, guzzling down a good ten ounces.

"I say go for it. Take it. Take what's yours!" I cheered, in a bad Scottish/Braveheart accent.

"I shall thrust my mighty sword into their stone!" He cheered back, in a bad English one. "Don't worry about me. I've got it covered. Tonight's going to be a good night." He clicked the TV on. *South Park.* A good sign.

We got to Seefeldt's house close to 11:00 p.m., fashionably late. By now Kyle and I had garnered a bit of a reputation in Bellgrove; he was cool with all of the potheads, and I was, well, I was that random dude who was banging Jules Levin. It was a fair labeling; I didn't make much effort to talk to anyone; my only concern was sneaking off with Jules to some empty room in the house. I guess I *had* been a bit selfish, in retrospect.

Kyle's buddies *hoorah'd* when he walked in, and lined up a beer bong for him.

"Ty, come on let's shotgun a brew!" Kyle shouted back to me. Jay-Z's, *"I Just Wanna Love U"* cut on, and the house cheered—bass banging through the walls. Everyone was hype; beer pong tables in the kitchen, crowds cheering and talking shit to each other; beach balls bouncing from one person to the next; the girls all had on tiny jean shorts and skimpy tank tops, fumbling around laughing with one another in their flip flops. *This was summer.*

I sliced through the aluminum Natty Light can with someone's car key, and circled up with Kyle and the rest of the shotgun crew.

"One… are you ready?" Kyle said to the dude in a neon pink tank top and backwards hat next to him, who was still struggling to key his beer. "Hurry up you pussy."

"Fuck you, Kyle," he shot back. Everyone laughed.

"Alright… ready…one-two-three-GO!" We all chugged, and I thought I was quick, but the fuckin kid in the pink tank top won by a landslide. I couldn't believe it.

"Haha! Suck my DICK!" he shouted. His victory dance looked like one of Allen's dance moves. "That's what I'm talkin' about! Pussieees!"

"Rematch! You fuckin cheated, I saw you take a head-start," Kyle said. "Ty, you saw that shit, didn't you?" he winked at me.

"Yep. Totally cheated. Rematch is the only way."

"Fuck you both, I just saw you wink at him, Kyle." Everyone was cracking up. Tank-top kid passed around another round of beers.

It felt great to hang with Kyle again, like old times, without petty arguments and billowing clouds of weed smoke.

Jules tugged my shirt.

"Tyler, *slow down*." She had one of her pouty-faces on, which was never good. I pulled her aside for a quick second.

"What's up, Deb?"

"Don't call me that."

"Listen, I haven't had a good drinking night with Kyle in forever. I won't get too wasted or pass out, I promise. You don't have to worry about me," I said.

"It's not you I'm worried about…" she said, eyes shifting to Kyle. I looked over to see him finish another beer bong in about 2.1 seconds flat. He seriously sucked it down at light-speed, and then fell backwards into the china cabinet, knocking over a few glasses. The whole house cheered.

"Hall in the house!" Tank-top screamed over the crowd. Kyle drunkenly raised his hand, signaling that he was ok, re-gaining his balance. They cheered again.

"Sometimes I think you're more in love with him than you are with me," Jules said.

"Oh come on, he's finally having a good time, *drinking* for once."

She frowned.

"Let's take a shot. Please? You need it…" I said, running off before she could slap or punch me.

We hit the makeshift bar in the living room. After a few drinks,

Jules was back to her normal self, and couldn't stop grabbing me, trying to pull me into the closet in the corner of the room. As much as I wanted to go with her, that night I just wanted to hang out with my long lost brother. I could see into the kitchen where Kyle was playing beer pong with tank-top kid. They were clearly running the table.

"Tylerrrrr," Jules whined, pulling my arm again.

"Jesus Christ, Jules would you get off me?" I said, shoving her aside. I immediately regretted pushing her, but I couldn't apologize now or I'd look like a bitch. So I walked off.

"Yo Kyle!" I screamed over the music. The kitchen was raging. There was a group of kids circling up around the balcony; it sounded like they were egging on some idiot who was about to go for the jump. *Fucking awesome.*

"What's up dude?" Kyle asked.

"Let's grab a beer," I said.

We hit the keg in the basement to fill our cups. His eyes were hardly hanging open. I needed to get on his level.

"No weed tonight," he said.

"Huh?"

"I didn't smoke tonight…" he said again, waiting for my response. I wasn't sure what to say, so I pumped the keg. "Thought you'd like to know is all," he said.

Again, I ignored the comment. I should've said something, but I couldn't find the words. I couldn't get my mouth to open. I should've said something like *I know, I noticed, thanks man* or, *I appreciate it bro, great to have a few beers with you* or, *I fuckin' miss you, Kyle. It really sucks without you.* Instead, I stared at the beer slowly swirling in my cup, averting eye contact for what felt like two and a half hours.

"You see any chicks out there?" I blurted out, trying to change the subject. He shrugged his shoulders. "Nothin'? Really?"

"Workin' on a couple, I guess," he said.

"Shit. Well let's go back up there then, you want me to wing man?" I asked.

"Nah it's cool. Where's Jules?" he asked.

"Not sure, actually. Somewhere around here."

"I'm probably gonna hit the hot tub with Richie and them," he said. I took a long sip of my beer, trying to hide my grin. "You know how gay that sounds right?"

He laughed. "We got some girls coming through."

And with that, the conversation died. Kyle walked back upstairs with his beer to rejoin his friends, and I stood by myself in that cold, damp basement. I could hear the crowd of cheers as he entered the kitchen. They loved him.

I realized there was no longer a real connection between the two of us; our childhood camaraderie was gone. It was a sobering moment, standing alone in the basement, with nothing but the shallow glow of a naked light bulb to offer me comfort. I was swallowed in darkness. *I let this happen.*

I went upstairs and found Jules, but I pushed her away again. I was consumed by this cacophony of shrieking loneliness; I had lost Kyle. I had blown it. He had moved on, found other friends. It was no longer me and him against the world. That reality *hurt*. I should've just said something downstairs when I had the chance.

Jules kissed me on the cheek.

"What's wrong?"

I didn't want to get into it.

"Tyler, talk to me." She was tugging at my arm, trying to get me to kiss her. I just wanted her to leave me alone for a while. I *wanted* to be angry. That's what drinking does to you; it lets you get out your aggression with no holds barred, and then fiercely regret it the next morning.

Kyle had been my best friend my entire life, and now it was

like none of it ever happened. I'd pushed him away and run off with Jules when I should have stopped and listened to him. There had to be a reason he always wanted to be high. *Was it me? Had he felt this way months ago?*

"You want a drink?" I asked Jules.

"We've already had enough," she said, grabbing my arm again. "Come on, let's go home."

I ripped my arm away from her.

"I'm getting another drink."

"Tyler…"

"Fuck off, Jules, really." I said.

I could see the heartbreak in her eyes, but I didn't care. I'd had enough heartbreak for one night. I turned my back to her and walked away.

*****

I must have dozed off. I remember jolting awake on the couch in the living room. The party was closing down; everyone was either fucking or passed out. The unlucky ones had gone home. The booze was gone and the lights were slowly flickering off. I tried to find Jules. I checked upstairs, the basement, and the backyard, but she was nowhere to be found. I kept searching for a good twenty minutes. I figured she must have walked home. I knew she was mad at me, but she wouldn't have stayed the night at Greg Seefeldt's house without me there with her.

She wasn't picking up her phone, so I left, staggering down side streets, focusing intently on making it back to her house. She had to be there. She must have called for a ride home, or walked back with some of her girlfriends. I was doing my best not to draw attention to my drunk self, zigzagging down the sidewalk.

As quietly as I could I snuck around Jules's house, peeking

through the windows and doors, but the place was completely dark with no sign of her. I cut back towards Kyle's grandfather's house. Maybe by some off-chance Kyle had walked her home, or vice a versa; she'd walked him. He was pretty wasted.

Stumbling through the cornfield for what felt like three hundred years, I finally caught sight of his grandfather's house. The moon was only a sliver in the sky, so I couldn't see much; only the faint outline of the house.

Then a floodlight kicked on. It was motion-censored, and now silhouetted two figures stumbling towards the door. It had to be Kyle and Jules. *Had* to be. Who else would be traipsing through the cornfield at this hour?

I called out, but it was useless, they were too far ahead of me and I didn't want to wake up the whole neighborhood, so I kept trudging along, trying to catch up. The damn cornfield was nearly a mile long. I trekked on, trying to focus on their shadows up ahead, but I was still significantly buzzed and the clumpy dirt made it impossible to keep my footing.

Before the shadows reached the house, they made a sharp turn left. I watched as the two of them slowly climbed the rope ladder up into the tree house, pulling the ladder up behind them. I could hear distant laughter; distinctly, Jules'.

Fuck. That. What, one fight and she's already running off with my best friend? What the hell were they doing up in the tree house at this hour? Kyle knew no one else could get up without that fucking ladder. Why the hell did he pull it up?

I heard more laughing and giggling as I approached. I started sprinting. My imagination was running wild with thoughts of Jules with him, climbing all over him, writhing on top of him. What kind of heartless bitch does something like this? Just runs off with another guy because of *one* small argument?

Shit. Had to stop sprinting, couldn't breathe.

I reached the tree house ten minutes later, exhausted and panting; wanting nothing more than to beat the hell out of Kyle, but also really wanting to just collapse on the ground and sleep. I nearly feel over. My hands were on my knees, I was dry-heaving and balancing myself on the trunk of the tree. I needed to start working out again. This was pitiful.

Then I heard it.

Muffled screams from inside of the tree house. *Jules' screams.* Not the good kind, either. There was nothing pleasurable about the noises she was making.

A light thumping reverberated the wood, all the way down the trunk to where I stood.

"*Shut the fuck up!*"

Kyle.

Jules was trying to fight him off. It sounded like she was trying to fight him back, but he was overpowering her. She kept trying to yell, but her cries were muffled. The thumping got louder, the pace picking up. I tried to find the rope ladder, fumbling around in the darkness. Then I remembered Kyle had pulled it up. That was no accident. Just as we had designed it, there was no way up into the tree house without that ladder.

The muffled screams grew softer as Kyle's grunts grew louder. I threw rocks, clumps of dirt, anything I could find, but it was useless.

"Kyle!" I screamed up into the tree house, stumbling backward. Nothing. Just more grunting and thrusting. I spotted a nearby tree and scrambled up into it; it was an easy climb, even drunk. I was hoping to catch a glimpse through the main window to try to figure out what the fuck was going on. I wish I hadn't. I was hoping I was interpreting these noises and this whole situation backwards and upside down. I wasn't.

What I saw, in the pale streaks of the moonlight, was Kyle

pinning down a beaten and bloodied Jules, thrusting himself into her like an animal. She no longer resisted, her head buried in a pillow, done with fighting. She couldn't win. I watched as he finished inside her, falling backwards onto the tree house floor in exhaustion.

Jules didn't move. She just cried. I could hear it from where I sat in that tree. I would hear it for the rest of my life.

CHAPTER EIGHTEEN

I woke up with bugs crawling in my nose, hungover, and confused. I had passed out in the cornfield. I couldn't remember how I got there. I couldn't remember anything after being in the tree, and seeing Kyle on Jules.

I called Jules, but she still didn't pick up. I went to her house, but she wouldn't see me, and her dad answered the door, which meant there was no way I was getting past him and inside to see her. Not to mention I was filthy and blatantly hungover; a stuttering, bumbling mess. I'd probably never be allowed to set foot in the house again.

I took the train home by myself. I didn't call Kyle, didn't look for his text, didn't want to even think about him. I was sick. I couldn't shake the images from last night. Standing at the trunk of the tree, not able to do anything to help. *Why didn't I wake up Kyle's grandfather? Or call the police? Or my grandparents? Anything* would have been better than what I did. I climbed a fucking tree, sat there, and watched. How did this whole thing even happen?

For a second I tried convincing myself that it was a dream,

but the images were too real. *Why did she go home with Kyle? What did he say to her?* That scumbag lured her into the tree house, laughing all the way, and then forced her to the floor and tore her clothes off. I was going to fucking murder Kyle the next time I saw him.

That night I got a call from Jules' mother. Her voice was flat and dulled. She told me Jules had killed herself.

CHAPTER NINETEEN

It was the first time I had told Jules' story since it happened. The first time since I'd stood on the stand in front of a packed court house and described in detail, to a room full of people I didn't know, what happened that night. I kept my back to Rachel, pressing my eyes shut, angry at their dampness.

"And then what happened?" Rachel asked. She was still sitting on the couch, with her notepad in her lap. Something about her had changed. She wasn't crying anymore. Her posture was erect.

"I made sure Kyle got what he deserved, and we buried Jules." I sucked it up and straightened myself out. I turned to her. "That's all that happened."

"Yeah…" she sighed. "That's great and all… but I need details. Specifics. The trial, the sentence, everything that happened after. The things you did… The people you did them to… How did it go down?"

She was flicking her pen against her cheek, making that water-droplet noise, half smiling.

"I should have fucking known, from the minute you walked up to me last night--"

"Yah, but… you didn't. So please, Tyler Clark, continue before I call my lawyer or—better yet, the cops! —And this time we can put *you* on the stand."

"It sounds like you already know everything that happened."

"But you are my source, and I need the firsthand account. Hearsay doesn't do much good to a reporter like me." She clicked on the tape recorder.

"How long have you worked for *The Inquirer*?" I asked.

"Long enough."

"Is this how you lure all of your contacts in? By promising them a good fuck?"

She uncrossed her legs, and spread them out a bit. "I didn't *promise* you anything. I *gave* it to you, Tyler."

I stared her down, long and hard.

"You've got a lot of dark secrets. I'm intrigued," she said. Her hair fell from her shoulders, suspended in midair. She brushed it back.

"Talk to me. Tell me about Victoria," she said.

Hell no. "I'm not falling for this bullshit." I said.

"I'm not asking you to. You'd better tell me something, because I'm running out of patience."

I just kept staring at her. She shrugged, all cute and innocent-like. The devil reincarnated.

"Just say the word…and I'm yours." She reached across the table, slowly, provocatively, and picked up her cell phone. She unlocked it and dialed. "Nine…one…one--"

"Stop! Ok, just stop." I had absolutely no control in this conversation. My only hope was to give her what she wanted. "Put the phone down and I'll tell you what happened."

She dropped the phone and giggled. *Click.*

Click click.

CHAPTER TWENTY

It was difficult to figure out how to fully comprehend what had happened, especially in the first few days after Jules's death. It hurt to think, so I didn't. I just moped around, day after day, hour after hour.

Time slowed to a crawl; I couldn't sleep, and the days never ended. Afternoons lasted an eternity. It was Hell. I played video games, watched crappy daytime television, ate when I could, and tried to sleep. I was unsuccessful at all of it.

I cried. I cried a lot. I cried during the day, I cried during meals, at night, at the movies, everywhere. My thoughts had a way of always getting the best of me. Everything reminded me of her, I couldn't escape it. *Everything*. The breeze, my food, a rock on the ground, the shoes on my feet—it didn't matter. They were all triggers. I learned to force myself to shut down. It was easier to pretend none of this ever happened. No tree house, no summer camp, no music, no Jules.

I hated it. I hated crying and I hated Kyle and I hated her. I hated her so much and I hated myself for it, but it wouldn't stop. My blood turned black, my heart was stone.

I couldn't for a *second* imagine what she must have gone through, the trauma, the horror. I couldn't stop thinking about those black eyes. Those piercing black eyes staring right through me, picking me apart piece by piece; tearing through my soul. I kept running conversations over in my mind, trying to imagine what he must have said to her, how he must have grabbed her and forced her to her knees. *What possibly could have been going on in his mind for him to act like that?* What did I do? I must have been Kyle's trigger. Who else? Our friendship had fallen apart and I hadn't been the nicest person in world to him in recent months, but he wasn't exactly a prince either. He was an asshole. *But I never called him out on it!* We only had a few arguments here and there. I wasn't confrontational. What could I have done to have made him so mad he would do that to her? It just didn't make sense. There's no way I could have upset him *that* much. No possible way.

And Jules. *What the fuck Jules?* You didn't have to go. I would have been there for you, every second of every day I would have consoled you, and held you, and loved you until you felt safe. I know it would take time, but I had all the time in the world to give to you. You were my life. *I loved you.*

If she loved me as much as she said she did in that goddamn letter, why did she kill herself? Because she's a fucking coward, that's why. A fucking spineless coward.

I take that back. *I'm so sorry for what happened, Jules.*

I'm so sorry.

*****

There was a massive investigation after Jules' death, and because I was addressed in her departing letter, the police showed up five squad cars deep at my doorstep with their guns drawn like I had personally assisted her in her death. They drug me into the police station every morning of that first week to regurgitate what I had "witnessed." I didn't fucking witness anything. If I knew she was going to do it, I would have fucking stopped it.

They made me retell my story to different officers, Police Chiefs, Detectives from my county, Bellgrove County, Philadelphia district, even the goddamn state troopers that patrolled the highways between my house and her grandparents'. It was a bit much, but then again, the government has always been great at overusing resources in the most unnecessary ways.

There were lawyers everywhere. Scumbag lawyers, creeping out of the woodwork, twisting your words around to fuck you over. They give you their smug smiles, poking and prodding, trying to catch you in your lies. I wasn't scared, I had nothing to hide. I told them everything. I blew that fucking whistle like it was my last breath.

I felt sick all the time. The reality of what had happened hadn't quite set in. I didn't know if it ever would, and it made me nauseous when I thought about it for too long. She had just been there. Now she was gone.

After about two weeks of blank stares and numb conversation with my sweetly empathetic grandparents, the anger set in.

Anger like this was new to me, and I had no idea how to handle it. I became incredibly violent. It was like my ten-year-old, hissy fit self had evolved into a scrawny man version, with a lot more strength than before and an exponential growth in unpredictability. I destroyed things. I only had to think about Kyle for *two seconds* and I would be smashing a hole in the wall with a table lamp, or kicking over the TV, beating my drum set, or swinging the cymbal stand like a baseball bat into a bookshelf. I didn't care that I was ruining my own stuff. It was all equipment I had saved to buy so that I could create music and tapes and

CDs with *Kyle Hall.* I wished he was that bookshelf I destroyed. I wished more than anything in the world that I would see him hop the fence into my backyard, so that I could kill him. I would tackle him, pin him down, and suffocate the life out of him with my bare hands. I would steal the last bit of light from those black eyes. Fortunately, or unfortunately, depending on how you look at it, this was not possible, because Kyle had been sent away to a juvenile correctional center downtown.

I fought hard in court. In Pennsylvania, the court is open to the public if the juvenile defendant is over the age of fourteen and charged with a felony offense. To hefty applause, I screamed and cursed, told the Judge and Kyle's lawyers to go fuck themselves, attested to Kyle's violent and drug-induced tendencies, and teared up with rage at every mention of Jules. I couldn't fucking help it. They had pictures of her everywhere as evidence, and everyone was talking about how beautiful she was on the inside and out. I kept seeing her face, her smile, and hearing her laugh. After about five minutes of boldly testifying my lawyer yanked me from the stand and kept me in my seat for the rest of the trial. I didn't care. I blamed Kyle for the rape. The evidence was clear; I saw what he did with my own eyes, and Jules' suicide note supported it. The coroner reported traces of Kyle's skin under Jules' fingernails; no doubt a result of her futile attempts to escape. We tried to bring Emma to the stand, but she refused to testify against her brother. Even after he dropkicked her out of a tree house and broke her arm and two ribs, she wouldn't do it.

My lawyer pummeled Kyle's State-appointed lawyer mercilessly into the ground during every debate, and in the end Kyle was charged with rape, which is somehow, in PA, a misdemeanor if you're a minor.

A fucking *misdemeanor*.

We argued that Kyle intentionally aided Jules to commit

suicide and therefore was guilty of a felony in the second degree; but because of the phrasing of a goddamn sentence in Jules' suicide note that Kyle's piece-of-shit lawyer twisted around, he convinced the jury that Kyle was in fact, not an aide in her suicide. In a fury, I opened up and blamed our entire marijuana operation on him, and cited his constant use of narcotics as a clear indicator for his unbelievable, irrevocable, sociopathic behavior.

Kyle didn't care. He was indifferent. He didn't once bat an eye or object to any of the accusations. He let his lawyer do the talking, and just stared at the state flag hanging motionless in the corner of the room. Probably wishing he had some more weed to smoke.

I told the jury what he'd done to his own sister, kicking her off a thirteen foot platform, but it was discarded as Emma would not admit the story to be true. We were at least able to convince the judge to issue a warrant for the DEA to raid Kyle's house, which they did, uncovering all of the dope and money we stashed in his basement, charging him with a first class felony for possession with intent to distribute.

The fact that a few grams of pot incurred a harsher punishment than *raping* a girl will never make sense to me. Kyle would never have to register as a sex offender, and his record could be expunged in five years. There exists the *Sex Offender Registration and Notification Act* (SORNA), that requires each state to implement registration and notification standards for juveniles adjudicated delinquent of certain sex offenses such as rape, but to date, only the state of Ohio has been deemed in compliance with SORNA. Kyle didn't rape Jules in Ohio.

So basically, before I would legally walk into a bar and buy a drink as a twenty-one-year-old US citizen, Kyle's record would be wiped clean. No one would ever know he raped the love of my life, which caused her to commit suicide.

Forgiveness would *never* touch my heart, not in a million

years.

The jury found him guilty on all accounts, and he was sentenced to the PICC—Philadelphia Industrial Correctional Center—to serve until his eighteenth birthday, at which time he would be reassessed and likely released.

CHAPTER TWENTY-ONE

Happiness is a choice. I wasn't a fan of depression; it's miserable, there's no sugar coating it. After days turned to weeks, and weeks turned to months, I realized it was time for me to take control for a change, and do things that made me feel good. I had hoped I could close this horrific chapter of my life and move on to a new one, so I took a job as a bus boy at the Philadelphia Tennis Club the summer before college. It changed my perspective on a lot of things…few for the better.

The historic mansion complex, now converted to a private clubhouse, consisted of the basement *Green Room*, the first floor Dining Hall, the second floor Ball Room, and a massive balcony that overlooked the tennis grounds. The courts were grass, not something you see often growing up in Philadelphia.

My crew was the Green Room crew; the lowest level. If it were the middle ages, I was the equivalent of a beggar peasant; the waiters, servants; the chefs, thieves. It was a train wreck down there. The women of the crew were sexually harassed; the chefs spat in dishes and served food they had dropped on the floor. The waiters stole money, and slinked around behind the manager's back as they pleased. I, for the most part, kept my head down and my mouth shut. It seemed like the safest option.

"Hey faggot, come here real quick." One of the other bus boys, Chris, led me from the kitchen out to the fire escape. "What are you doing tonight after work?"

"Not much," I said.

"You should come drinking with us."

"Who is 'us'?"

"Me and Mick and the boys upstairs. We're heading to Sarah's party." Other than his constant referrals to me as a "homo," or a "dick sucker," Chris seemed like a pretty cool kid; he had a solid head on his shoulders from what I could tell, and seemed to know his way around the politics of the restaurant staff. I nodded my head. "Cool. You just gotta help me get the booze," he said.

"Sure."

"Come on." He heaved himself up onto a dumpster and leaped onto the fire escape ladder, hauling himself up and climbing to the next platform up. He looked back down at me expectantly. "Jump up! Let's go."

I followed him up the cold iron bars until we reached the third floor platform. There was a small window next to the door, which he pushed open and climbed in.

The window dropped into the club's liquor storage room. Boxes lined the walls, littering the floors with cases of Belvedere, Absolute, Jameson, Beefeaters, and Black Label. We feasted our eyes for a few minutes. More booze than any eighteen year old could dream of having access to.

"Grab two Jamesons," he said, plucking out a Jack Daniels and two Absolutes. He unlocked the main door to the room and we stashed the bottles in the broom closet not far down the hall. We circled back down the fire escape, through the Green Room, and back up the rear staircase to the third floor. Chris jammed the bottles into a few "to-go" bags and hustled them out to the trunk of his car.

This became our weekly routine.

"Old man Nichols can't keep count of much, let alone alcohol inventory. He never notices the bottles are missing."

"How long have you been doing this?" I asked.

He shrugged. "Been here three years."

* * * * *

Sarah's party was a house party in a shady row-home in West Philly. I'm talking the low 50's of West Philly…It's not exactly prime real estate. Chris and I rolled in around midnight; the party was already raging.

"Alright! *This is a fuckin' party!* Do me a favor and don't be such a fuckin' bone smuggler tonight, alright? Plenty of fags you can hose down on your own time. Tonight, you came here with me, and we have an impression to make." He slapped me on the back and walked off. "Find us some women!"

I was embarrassed to be associated with Chris, so I headed in the only safe direction I could think: to the keg.

"Give us a pump, will yah?" I looked up to see a long-haired Irish guy staring at me, motioning to the keg I was hovering over. I pumped the lever a few times as he filled his cup. He was talking to an incredibly hot brunette—and I mean *incredible*—with cutoff jean shorts that would have served her well as a bathing suit; her tanned ass was hanging halfway out, and it jiggled when she shifted her weight. I looked up and she was staring right at me. *Shit*. I pumped the keg tap again and started whistling, and then acted like I received a text message. After a few seconds, I looked back up. She was gorgeous. She looked back over at me again. Thankfully this time she smiled before walking off.

"Do I know you?" the Irish guy said.

"Don't think so."

"You look incredibly familiar. Where do you come from?"

"I came with Chris..." I had forgotten Chris' last name. I'm not sure I ever knew it, actually. "We work at the Tennis Club."

"I didn't ask where ya *worked;* I asked where you're from."

"Philly." I said.

"No shit, we're all from Philly."

His Irish accent was so thick it was hard to understand him. "Overbrook," I said, extending my hand. "Tyler Clark."

"Jack West," he shook it. "You ever been to one of Sarah's parties?"

"First one," I said.

"Ah. And you said you came with Chris?" I nodded. "Have you met anyone else?"

"Not yet," I said. "Chris isn't the best at introductions."

"Chris is a bit of a cunt."

I couldn't help but laugh.

"Come upstairs with me for a minute, we'll have the craic. I want you to meet some people," he said.

On the way upstairs, I ran into Chris and introduced him to Jack. I kinda forced Chris to come along with us. As friendly as Jack seemed, I wasn't going anywhere with him alone in this house party in the hood of West Philly.

We settled in one of the upstairs bedrooms where four girls, including the hot-jean-booty-shorts girl, were waiting for us.

"Ladies! Sorry to have kept you waiting," Jack said, beaming a huge smile. They all giggled. "This here is my new friend Tyler, and you all know Chris."

"Nice to meet you," I stuttered out. The hotness of these girls was on another level, and one of them, with dark red hair and smooth skin, couldn't keep her eyes off me. I wanted to nonchalantly move closer her, so I started looking for a place to take a seat, but there weren't many openings, so I jammed my hands in my pockets and kind of just stood there. She flashed a smile at me. I reciprocated. Jack brought a tray of filled shot glasses and handed them out.

"Sláinte!" he shouted.

Everyone tossed back the vodka shot. As the alcohol took off through my bloodstream, I decided to go for it. I went for the tiny little space next to the red haired girl; they had circled up on the floor in a little pow-wow. I mumbled something inaudible and pointed at the open spot on the rug. She smiled and moved over to make room.

When I sat down I felt that electric pulse, that instantaneous human connection with her. I *loved* that, knowing when a girl likes you. It's thrilling. I felt like I was back at camp, huddled around the fire. Then Jack pulled out a zip-locked baggie of white powder and plopped it on the table, and I realized this was definitely not going to be like camp. The girls shrieked in excitement.

"Alright! I like this guy, Ty," Chris said to me, his eyes transfixed on the bag. I could feel the red head looking at me, trying to judge my reaction. In all honesty, I was fucking pissed. This was bullshit. I didn't want to be in a room with a bunch of cokeheads snorting coke. I wasn't a cokehead.

I watched them as they took turns furiously inhaling their "magic white." One by one, sucking in hard, tilting their heads back, laughing as their eyes watered up from the burn. *What was I doing here? I wasn't a cokehead...*

Kyle's face flashed in front of me. I could see him cowering in the corner with his drugs. He was always *so high*, laughing hysterically at the stupidest things, like penis-shaped clouds in the sky. But the more I thought about it, the more I questioned: who was happier? Me, or Kyle? I knew the answer, but Kyle didn't deserve to be happy; *I* did. I wanted to be fucking happy for a change. Besides, you aren't a cokehead if you just do it once, right? Just to try it, to tick off that little square box and never worry about it again, right? Maybe living this way *was* better. Why can't I escape from it all, too? Fuck taking the high road. Fuck always making the responsible choice. A lot of good that did.

"I'm Lisa," the redhead said. We locked eyes and she smiled, and then I got embarrassed and looked down. *What the hell happened to my confidence?* I had it a second ago when I sat down next to her. This dumbass cocaine business was throwing me off my game. I was inexperienced with it and unprepared for this situation, and I was retreating, turning into an angry buzz kill. Why couldn't everyone just take shots and drink beer like normal people? Why do drugs and weed and pills *always* have to come out and ruin the fun?

I thought of Kyle again, sucking away at his filthy little bong in the corner, like Sméagol with his precious ring, inhaling the thick white smoke with tremendous force. I could hear his obnoxious cackling laugh and his bold new ideas; concocting, conspiring.

Then I thought of Jules kicking the goddamn bucket—cutting her beautiful life away from herself without even a second thought. And it was all because of Kyle.

"Tyler," Lisa said again, snapping me out of it. She was holding a rolled up dollar bill out for me to take it. Everyone was staring at me. It was my turn; last in line.

Fuck it. Let's see what this bullshit was all about. I snorted back a line, hard and fast.

Oh my god.

I felt like the alpha. I was cool, but not in a popularity kind of way. In an *I've got this shit figured out and these motherfuckers don't know the half of it* kind of way. It was poetry. I was *me*. *Me* in the ultimate sense of what *I* could be. I was the lead actor in the most badass movie ever, and everyone in this little circle was here for my monologue. They *needed* to know what I was thinking. They needed to know how I approached life, because it was the best and only way. Everything else was utterly trivial. I had to help them. I could have written a book in the fifteen minutes that passed. I turned to Lisa and explained to her everything about anything that crossed my mind, and she listened like her life depended on it, because it did; she would be lost without me, you know? I was here to guide her through this world. She kept looking at me, licking her lips, playing with her necklace, rubbing her thighs. I needed to quickly convince her that now was the time, in the room across the hall, with the door closed. *Our* time.

Fucking Lisa was like fucking a porn star in a helicopter as I flew over Mount Fiji firing a .60-caliber machine gun at a sea of hostiles while the sun dropped over the hills, except I was on the bathroom floor with my head banging against a filthy toilet and my jeans hanging halfway off my ass. Didn't matter. Had sex. *WINNING*.

Then I woke up in a pool of what smelled like vomit in the middle of a dark, cold, war prison with hacked open plastic milk containers filled with piss and shit stewing in the corners, and a nauseating hunger that couldn't be fed.

Luckily the vomit was only in the sink, and it wasn't mine. I pulled up my pants and told Lisa I would be right back.

I stumbled over to the bar area and took another shot of whiskey whilst filling up another solo cup of beer. Partying like a rock star was harder than it sounded. I guess if being wasted all the time were easy, everyone would do it. I sat down in a blue,

Lay-Z-boy chair and kicked off my shoes (I knew the rules; hell if I was going to wake up with dicks drawn in permanent marker on my face). I couldn't remember where Lisa was, but it didn't really matter, and I didn't care. It had been a good night, and I was ready to get to sleep.

CHAPTER TWENTY-TWO

One afternoon that next week, Irish Jack called me. I guess I had given him my number the night of Sarah's party.

"Tyler, what the fuck is up, mate?" He sounded in a good mood.

"Oh...hey, what's up Jack?" I tried to hide my lack of enthusiasm. Probably not as well as I'd hoped.

"Meet me at Cuddy's, let's grab a beer."

* * * * *

Two cold IPAs slid in front of us.

"How was your time with Lisa?" Jack asked me with a smirk.

"From what I can remember...pretty amazing."

"She said the same about you."

Now I was the one smirking.

"What are your plans for the fall?" he asked.

"Heading off to Penn State."

"Ah. To pursue your dreams as a musician?"

"Electrical engineering, actually." I threw back a swallow of beer. Few things excited me less than the thought of electrical engineering at Penn State. I damn well didn't even know why I applied for it. Good scores on the math section of my SATs, I guess.

"And what of your music?" he asked.

"It's a hobby."

"Shouldn't be."

"It's a lot harder than it may seem. Record deals aren't exactly a dime a dozen."

He furrowed his brow and drank. I could almost *see* his mind at work.

"What if I told you I could get you one?"

"I'd ask...what's in it for you?" Was this guy serious? Did he know someone?

He laughed. "I like you. A skeptic, and rightfully so. It's not often that a pot-dealing musician fights his way through a rape case and still has the energy to keep swinging."

How the fuck did he know about that?

"How do you know about that?" I glared.

"You're quite the talkative lad after a few bumps. You should be more careful."

Jesus. "Thanks for the beer," I said, pushing my barstool back to leave.

"Tyler, wait," he said. I stopped. "I don't have the connections to put a record deal on your lap, but I do have the skills you'll need to get to those who do. You're a good kid, you've got a big heart and a lot of fight in you, I can tell. I didn't have the easiest childhood either, but those who've seen the worst often become the best. I'd like to see you succeed."

I was waiting for him to tell me what he wanted in return.

"All I ask for in return is that you let me use you as a case study. I'm in the Master's Program at Temple University. I'd like you to be my thesis study."

I wasn't expecting that. I was expecting some trick to get me to pay him, or to give him a percentage of my music revenue, or to be my manager, or agent, or some bullshit of which I would swiftly decline. This actually sounded pretty cool.

"What do you have in mind?" I asked, slowly putting my jacket back on the bar chair.

Jack smiled and signaled to the bartender for another round. "As a future psychologist, I'd like to teach you the art of persuasion."

*****

We met up twice a week at different coffee shops and pubs around town. I had homework assignments, textbooks to read, and papers to write; it was like taking a class and, unlike anything I had learned in high school, it was extremely useful. It was the most practical, beneficial, and flat out fun class of my life.

Rhetoric truly is an art. Jack showed me the light. It was like mastering a dark art; we tapped into the subconscious of others in order to get them to do what we wanted them to do. It was like hypnosis without the couch, the doctor, and his pocket watch with the forever-swirling black & white circle. It was everything Kyle had been a master of without realizing it. Some are born with the skills of discourse. Others are taught.

Jack was one of the lucky ones born with the skill to persuade. He realized early on, and took the initiative to "enhance" his skill set by practicing all through his teenage years. By the time he was twenty, he had graduated early with a BS in Sociology from a Pennsylvania state school. Having a knack for sales, he went into the insurance business where he made a small fortune. He decided to return to school to get a master's degree so that he could escape the sales world and apply for the more prestigious jobs in the industrial organizational psychology field. It was his dream, at least for the moment, and a hard feat without the right paperwork. A PhD was pretty much standard.

He loved the stuff. You could see it in his eyes, in his smile, in the way he carried himself. He loved being able to manipulate anyone he pleased. He was a master; to the point where those he chose became convinced his ideas were their own. It was like the movie *Inception*, where Leo hacks into someone's subconscious while they dream and implants an idea of his own. Jack's method was much more possible, and a whole lot faster; he could flip you in a five minute conversation, sitting right there in front of your face, smiling, laughing, plotting. It was brilliant.

We started with the simple stuff. First impressions start with the first word and the first physical contact, even if that's something as simple as shaking hands. The difference between a firm handshake and the dead-fish shake is astounding, as is making eye contact versus looking off nervously. Crossing your arms during a conversation versus sitting comfortably with them outstretched sends a completely different message. *Your* movements affect your opponent's. For example, you could open them up and make them feel comfortable simply by leaning back in your chair and cracking a few relatively profane jokes, or you could close things down and play into an uncomfortable hostility at the table by posturing dominance. *You* control the flow. The right body language and eye contact was the difference between getting a girl to go home with you that night, and failing to even let her buy you a drink.

The textbooks he had me read were amazingly insightful. They were upper-levelers written by gaudy Harvard professors and chock full of technical jargon, but when you simplified it to layman's terms, it wasn't impossible stuff to understand. Little things like smiling, remembering the person's name, expressing a genuine interest, and *knowing what they want* make a world of difference. What's incredible is that all of this knowledge is right there, in the local library, available to anyone who wants it, and yet, so few people take the time to explore it. A couple of trips to the library and you'd be par with master's students. But I guess it's no different from people who complain about their out-of-shape figures but aren't willing to put in the time at the gym; or people who hate their jobs but are too scared to go out and apply for another one. No one is holding them back but themselves. Their loss.

Jack wasn't just book smart. *Those who can, do; those who can't, teach*—was his favorite saying. We would prepare all week and then test out what I'd learned that weekend at the bar or the pizza shop or the mall. At first he led by example: we would head into a shoe store and he would work his magic until the manager gave me a sixty percent discount on a pair of sneaks. We would go into Victoria's Secret stores and Jack would hit on the girls working there, except it wasn't *hitting* on them, it was easier than that. It was just a small conversation about the price of a piece of lingerie and, with the right flick of the wand—or the right flash of a smile and light touch to her arm—he had her giving him a tour of the entire store and her business card with her cell phone number written on the back, asking him to "call her with any questions." Within a few weeks, I was right in there with him. We ran the story that we were brothers, reunited after Jack was shipped away to Ireland as a mere infant.

It wasn't long before girls became too easy. Once you knew *what* they were looking for and how desperately they were looking for it, it was like taking candy from a baby. The real challenge was in the workplace, with your boss, a colleague, or…with someone you just met and want to make a great first impression with, so they'll sign you to a record deal.

In order to get your feet wet you have to go to the water. In my case, the water source was the record label. *A* record label. *Any* record label. The trouble was, I only had a week left before I shipped out to Penn State to start school, and Jack's summer semester was coming to a close.

I decided it could wait. I wasn't going to let music leave my life; Jack and I both knew it. He was the catalyst I'd needed. He propelled me out of my lull and back into the studio, and for the first time in a long time, I was excited about music again. Jack was a dreamer, and had plans to help see mine through even if it killed us both. We'd had a great summer together. We drank, studied, persuaded, and bagged a lot of chicks. A *lot* of chicks. I pushed my personal record into double digits that last weekend before college; a tiny little blond chick named Laura on Friday, and this cute Asian girl on Saturday.

CHAPTER TWENTY-THREE

College was better than I thought it would be. My roommate, Tom Growling, was the man. He was tall and lanky, always cracking hilarious jokes, walked-on the PSU baseball team, and had a gift for picking the right parties to go to. The first night we split 750mL of Absolute vodka I nicked from the tennis club. Needless to say, I don't remember much of that night, but every night following it was dope. Jack West's lessons served me well, and I passed a few tricks on to Tom, not that he really needed them. We made out pretty well that semester, and I managed to even maintain a 3.6 GPA. *Dean's list.*

Over winter break, I went back into the studio to record my debut solo album. To my pleasant surprise, my music had started to gain some momentum online. YouTube had just launched, and it was pretty easy to become popular if you made the right moves—it wasn't as flooded as it is today. I didn't do much, just uploaded a few of my songs so that everyone could listen to them, but it was enough, and it worked. The videos I'd done had thousands of views; my most popular songs had over ten thousand.

I decided to write the album entirely on my own; I didn't want to shuffle around on the crutches of *Run of the Mill* anymore, and I didn't want to give Kyle an ounce of credit for anything. He deserved to rot in jail.

But as hard as I tried, and with as many songs as I wrote, none of them compared to what Kyle and I had created. None of them came close. I soon gave up my valiant efforts to write the damn songs myself and cut a ten song album entirely of *Run of the Mill* songs.

I had nightmares about Kyle that winter. I was turning nineteen in a month, which meant he was out of juvie by now. Out there somewhere, lurking in the darkness, like the rapist he was. In the back of my mind I feared he was hunting me down—waking from his bed at 4:00 a.m. in a cold sweat dreaming of revenge, tracking me down in some twisted delusion of vengeance. Or maybe he wasn't, maybe he had come to terms with his sins and found God.

My terrors spread from night to day that next semester; I would imagine seeing him as I walked to class, studied at the HUB, jammed onto the Blue Loop. I could see him, slinking behind the bushes with some rusty old dagger, waiting for his perfect opportunity to strike. No matter what, I always envisioned him with a rusty dagger. Like the old guy from Aladdin with skinny legs, crooked teeth, and crazy bulging eyes.

I had all but forgotten about him in the last few months. I wanted to keep it that way, but recording the album wouldn't let me. Things were bigger and better than anything we'd ever done for *Run of the Mill*; the studio was massive and had top of the line equipment. I brought in professional musicians to play and focused on the intricacies of the production more carefully. Naturally, as every artist does, I second-guessed myself the entire two months it took to track. Still, it was a ton of fun to record.

I wanted this album to outdo our *Run of the Mill* CDs in every way possible, and I knew it would.

With the release of the new album, I decided it was time to get another band together, so I used my Jack West skills to wrangle together a group of musicians willing to play for me for free. If you promise a man all the gold his heart desires, he'll go to war with you. One mention of my pursuit of a record deal, combined with an extremely convincing follow up pitch on how the deal was only a few weeks away as I was in talks with a couple of the labels *right now*, and I had a band. It wasn't lying, it was stretching the truth. I *was* in talks with the labels… they just hadn't talked back yet.

We played in various pubs as often as we could get booked, which peaked at once a month. We put on a good show. Most patrons were there to watch football games, but the bartenders were always bobbing their heads and applauding. *Tyler Clark* mixed with *Run of the Mill*, with some Led Zeppelin and Ben Folds Five thrown in there.

One particularly chilly Monday night in March, a group of freshman girls stopped in at the pub for a few drinks. March Madness, the college basketball tournament, had just ended the weekend before, so the bar was virtually empty. Back to normal for us.

We were in the middle of the solo section of "Dazed and Confused" when she caught my eye. As soon as I saw her I knew I had to have her; she had dirty blonde curly hair that dropped down to her shoulders, and a body that had me nearly doing backflips on stage. She had a figure similar to Jules, but a little taller and a bit more in all of the right places. I could tell from her body language and eye contact that she was interested in me.

Feeling particularly confident after crushing my reverse-engineering exam earlier that day, and after putting on a solid second set with the band, I pursued *little miss Jules lookalike* during our break. The eye fucking had been going on for long enough; it was time to go in for the kill. Hesitation in situations like that can and will destroy you. Generally speaking, you should always abide by the five-second rule. You have to strike as soon as the opportunity presents itself. When you see the girl, you've got five seconds to talk to her or you've failed the game. It makes you look a million times more confident than you actually are. For shy guys like my former self, it forces you to man up.

"You guys look like you're having a good time," I said. "Can I squeeze in for a beer?"

"Oh yes you can!" One of the girls in her gang chirped from the back. They all looked at Dirty Blonde and smiled. It was obvious they were waiting for me to come over, they could barely contain themselves, and Dirty Blonde was now blushing. The bartender slid a round of shots in front of them, so I canceled my beer and ordered one more shot, joining in.

"Your songs are amazing."

"Thank you," I smiled at Dirty Blonde, "it's good to have an audience as pretty as all of you." A few of them blushed. "I'm Tyler," I said.

"Victoria," Dirty Blonde said, shaking my hand, holding on for a few seconds longer than normal.

"That's a pretty name," I said, grabbing my guitar from my bassist as he walked by. I didn't want to come across as desperate, so I threw a wrench in the convo. "I've got to head off and take the boys here home." I tossed a couple bills on the bar to pay for my shot. You could see the disappointment in Victoria's eyes. "But I'll probably have a few drinks back at my place after… you should come with me. You guys are all welcome to come," I said to the group. They immediately turned down my offer, but nudged Victoria off with huge smiles. I gave them each hugs, invited them out to my next show, and left with Victoria.

*****

We were just getting settled when Tom came stumbling in, hammered drunk. He couldn't have had worse timing.

"Bitches, bitches!" he screamed.

I shielded Victoria from his helicopter blade arms as he twirled himself in circles, rambling on in slurs about how some girl had told him he was in the wrong room.

"She kept saying *'get out! Get out you pervert!'* And I couldn't for the life of me figure out why. She had just invited me up to her room; we were hooking up at the frat."

"Which frat?" I asked.

"Alpha Sig."

"Ah. Nice," I said. I needed to end this conversation as soon as possible.

"The room was so bright though. With those fluorescent ceiling lights, you know?"

"All dorm rooms have fluorescent ceiling lights, Tom," I said, pointing to our ceiling.

"Yeah, but this one had like ten of them in a row, and a bunch of sinks. It was like a bathroom."

It sounded to me like he had literally walked into a girls' bathroom and had been kicked out, but I couldn't tell for sure, and I didn't care to stick around long enough to decipher his mumbling. He was jumping from bed to bed now pretending to be a monkey, and while it was mildly entertaining, it was not as good as what Victoria and I were about to get into, so we left. But not before Tom threw up in his mini trashcan, and then passed out on his bed.

I apologized to Victoria about a million times, made sure Tom was positioned on his side in case he barfed again, and left.

"Maybe we should call it a night," Victoria said, pressing the "down" elevator button.

"No! No, I'm really sorry about that. He can get a little out of control. Let's go grab a drink at the pub down on College Ave."

"I only have a fake state ID, it doesn't scan," she said.

"How about I grab the bottle from my room and we'll just hang out downstairs?" I recommended. She gave me a forced smile, hinting towards a 'no thanks', but I ignored it and ran off to get my handle of vodka. She was so hot; I didn't want her to go.

After a few more drinks and a couple shots, she had forgotten about Tom's antics earlier, and we were back to having a blast. The lounge was empty, and I had cut all of the lights off except for a strand of Christmas lights that hung from the wall over the bulletin board. The soft, warm glow set the perfect mood.

I moved in next to her on the couch. She was talking about some character in a novel she was reading, which made me want her even more because she wasn't some bird-brained self-proclaimed model like so many other girls at this school. She actually read books. *Books!*

"Victoria," I said, interrupting her. She looked at me with her beautiful brown eyes and that amazing smile. I decided to hit her with the surprise approach, so I closed my eyes and kissed her. Her lips were soft and gentle, and we fell into a perfect rhythm. I massaged her with my left hand; my fingertips calloused from my guitar. Our breathing grew heavier, and she started that sine-like pulsing motion with her hips. I slowly slid my left hand down towards her belt.

"No," she whispered.

"What's wrong?" I said.

"Not tonight."

I smiled, hiccupped, and brought my hand back up. "Ok."

We kissed passionately. She stopped, leaned back, grabbed the vodka bottle and took a long, hard swig. I shuttered just watching her take it. Then she passed it to me, and I did the same. We stared into each other's eyes for a minute. I tapped my fingers lightly on her stomach in a drumming pattern.

"You're quite the musician, aren't you?" she said with a grin. I said nothing and kissed her. I loved kissing her. The excess alcohol made its way into my bloodstream. The TV flickered behind us, and we kissed into the night.

Then I woke up.

CHAPTER TWENTY-FOUR

The room was bright. The walls were whitewashed with sunlight, my vision was blurry, and my brain pounded against the walls of my skull. Posters of Marilyn Monroe, shirtless Johnny Depp and Russell Crowe lined the walls. Everything had a pink hue to it. Even the sheets I was lying on were tinted. This wasn't my room. This had to be Victoria's.

My eyes finally adjusted. I let out a groan and looked around. A yelp pierced my ears from the far corner of the room. Victoria stood huddled against the door of her closet, gripping a thin piece of molding she had ripped off of the door frame. She looked pale and horrified. *Horrified by the sight of me.*

Her hair was a mess, half covering her face, and I could tell she had been crying. I pushed myself up with my arms into a pushup position to see her more clearly.

"Hey. Are you ok?" I asked. My head was killing me. "Why are you crying?"

Then I saw what I was laying on. Her white sheets had bloodstains all over them. My drunken haze disappeared instantly. *What the fuck… happened?*

I looked back up at Victoria, and got out of bed. She screamed, gripping her splintered sword so tight I thought her hands would bleed.

My boxers had blood on them, and underneath my boxers was soaked even more.

"Vict--"

"Stay away from me!" She shrieked, like a threatened animal backed in her corner.

"What happened?" I asked. I was beginning to feel as frightened as she looked.

"You know exactly what happened," she said. I couldn't remember a fucking thing, but I had a sinking inclination as to what probably went down. "I'm calling the police. My dad, and my brother, and my friends are going to *kill you!* You fucking piece of shit! GET OUT!" She was hysterical now.

"Hold on! Please. Give me one second. Are you ok?"

I asked genuinely, but it came out contrived.

"I'm calling the police!" she screamed, picking up her phone.

"Ok. Ok…ok, but just wait, just one second, please…" I pleaded, taking a step towards her. She dropped the phone upon seeing me approach, and cocked the molding like a baseball player at the plate.

Was this really happening? The last thing I could remember was kissing this amazing girl on the couch, wanting to just curl up and fall asleep next to her under the glow of those twinkling Christmas lights. I wanted to wake up and laugh it off, both hungover from the drinks and the lust, and walk her home. Probably grab a cup of coffee on the way. Ask if I could take her on a date later that week, out to dinner, or to one of those free concerts the school was always throwing. There was an a cappella group coming on Wednesday. I wanted to get to know her. I wanted to fall in love with her. Not…this.

Had I really done it? I couldn't remember a goddamn thing from last night after taking that last swig from the bottle, and it was driving me mad. My head was about to explode, and the more I tried to recollect the night before, the harder my brain rammed against my skull.

"I told you *no*," she whimpered, tears streaming. "GET OUT!"

This was fucked up. Fucked up for sure. But I was not going to court, and I was not going to jail. I didn't do this. I would *never* do this.

I couldn't fucking think straight, and I started to panic. The reality of it all was creeping in. Whatever had happened, whether I thought I was capable or not, *happened*. In court, it would be her word against mine. If she went to the police today, they would swab her down and find my DNA all over her. The entire lower section of my torso was *bloody*. This was so fucked up.

I immediately thought about Jules. I thought about how she had screamed for Kyle to stop. Kyle Hall, scumbag of the universe. The kid I had spent my entire childhood with, who turned into a monster, whom I sent away to prison. I wanted to *kill* Kyle for what he had done. And now here I stood, guilty of the same crime. I had become everything I despised.

But I wasn't headed for juvie; I was an adult, and I was headed for *prison*, for a long, long time. My collegiate career was over. My music career was over. My life was over.

As I stood there lost in thought, out of the corner of my eye I caught Victoria picking up her phone again to dial the police.

That's when something inside of me snapped.

I was not going to prison. My life was *not* ending today because of *one* girl and this *one* fucked up situation that *may or may not have actually happened* and that I couldn't even fucking remember. Besides, what if she faked this? What if she knew about my music and wanted to get rich quick by charging me with rape and creating a huge scandal in hopes that I would fold and settle outside of court for a huge fee? She *did* come to my show, and she made it extremely obvious that she wanted to hang out with me afterwards. It was possible, right? No, it was *probable*.

And fuck this girl in particular—*Victoria*—if that was even her name. She was probably out to get me from the minute she walked into the bar last night, if not earlier. She'd probably had this whole thing planned for the past year and a half... the minute after I released my first album she discovered me and applied to the same college as me so that she could find me and fuck me over. I didn't deserve this. I was just trying to live my life, and here this girl comes to ruin it.

"Put the fucking phone down," I said.

She jumped a little, and dropped the phone back on her desk.

This was my show now.

"Let me tell you something, Victoria." I said. I pointed around the room as I slowly shuffled towards her. "This whole... *situation* we have here... this never happened. *We* never happened. I don't know what ideas you've got running around in that fucked up little head of yours, but it sure as hell isn't anything you're going to talk about. *Ever.* You're not going to tell *anyone* I was here. You're not going to tell anyone about any of this, *ever*. Not your father, not your brother, not your friends, not the police." I was a few feet away from her now; making sure each menacing step I took was as poignant as the last. "If you think you can tell them and get away with it, let me tell you how wrong you are. I will come back for you, and I will fuckin' kill you."

She dropped the molding to the floor. Her entire body was trembling.

"You think this is bad? Test me. I *dare* you." I was inches from her face now. I put both my arms up on the wall behind her, staring dead into her eyes. My eyes were black. "Do you understand me?"

"Yes," she mumbled, eyes to the floor, tears falling from the brim of her nose.

"*What* are you going to do?" I asked.

"…Nothing," she stammered.

"Good."

I walked back to her bed and ripped the bloody sheets off, bundling them up under my arm. I dressed, grabbed my phone and wallet, took one last look at the room, and left without another word.

I knew she wouldn't say anything.

I drove out about forty miles on the main road into the Northeastern Pennsylvania countryside, and turned down an abandoned dirt path. I parked off on the side, out of sight of anyone driving past, and cleared a small area in the field. I lit a fire and burned the sheets and my bloody boxers.

*****

Back in my dorm, I took a long, hot shower, and washed my clothes four full times. I couldn't eat; all I managed to keep down was half a bottle of water. I tried fresh air; I walked a few blocks until I felt nauseous and had to stop. Then, like a brick, the exhaustion hit me. I slept the rest of that day.

CHAPTER TWENTY-FIVE

Thankfully, summer was around the corner. A few weeks later I packed up my dorm, and happily turned my back to Happy Valley. I needed to get the hell out of there. The guilt was unbearable. Every minute of every day for *weeks* I was haunted by the venomous words I shot at Victoria. The death threat monologue I had delivered with searing hatred to a trembling, violated, nineteen-year-old girl.

My mind was seized with terror. I was terrified that my threats wouldn't hold up, and that I'd find myself back in court again; this time as the defendant. I could barely eat. I threw up. I quit going to the gym. I was scared to check the mail, fearing the delivery of some notification from the district courts informing me that I was being charged.

Victoria's face was beginning to fade from my memory, which was a small comfort. The actual events of that night were never clear. Anything I *had* remembered was now consolidated into a blur. But I didn't for one second forget what I said.

I would never forget.

*****

The first few weeks home, I told my grandparents I was working on my second album, and needed time alone in my room to concentrate. I didn't actually record anything. I couldn't bear the sight of them; they reminded me of everything good in the world, and of how I was the complete opposite; I didn't deserve to be in their presence.

I shut myself out from everyone I knew; all of my high school friends home for the summer, neighbors, musician colleagues. I didn't want to show my face. I *couldn't* show my face. Contrition is hardly a strong enough word. I had betrayed myself. I had done the unthinkable.

I found some solace in drinking, so I ran with it. I drank a case of beer or a fifth of vodka daily. The alcohol slowed down my mind. It let me forget. It allowed me to focus entirely on whatever menial task I was doing for a few hours, like playing video games or watching movies, without my mind wandering off to Victoria, or Jules, or Kyle.

I passed the days watching movies or marathon watching television shows. My local library had a free movie rental policy, so each morning I woke up, drank a couple beers to get started, walked up to the library and rented a gang of films, hit the beer distributor so I'd have supply for the next day, and then locked myself back in my room until morning.

My body started to disintegrate. I'd quit working out weeks ago and I wasn't eating well, and on top of that I put my liver on its deathbed. My vision would sometimes blur uncontrollably for a few minutes, and more than once I lost hearing in one ear for the course of a day. Then the vomiting started, and I physically couldn't drink anymore. My system was rejecting the alcohol, and I couldn't get drunk. I fell into a cycle of malicious daydreams; killing Victoria to keep her quiet, or murdering Kyle for what he'd done, or finding Jules and killing her again just so that she could pay for the pain she'd caused me in killing herself.

I started suffocating myself, just to black out for a few minutes, to escape my tortured mind. I would sit against my bed and clutch my throat until I passed out. Then I'd wake up with a horrible headache and spotty vision, and do it again.

I plotted my suicide. I was too scared of a violent way out. I wanted to go easily. Cutting myself, hanging myself, or jumping in front of a train was too risky, too painful, and had too much room for error. I decided pain pills were the way to go, and bought a bottle of Vicodin from this pill-head kid named Brian I knew from high school. It cost me two hundred dollars for the whole damn bottle. He was definitely making a killing selling them. I had to steal the money from Granddad's emergency cash fund he stashed underneath his cigar boxes.

I drafted my letter over the course of a few days. I couldn't decide whether or not to confess to what I had done to Victoria, or to just blame Kyle again for ruining my life. Jules' blood was already on his hands. I figured mine could add to his burden. I prayed every night that his life be filled with pain and misery just like mine. I was convinced it was because of him that I had done what I did to Victoria. There was no other explanation, no other logical reasoning as to why I would behave that way other than because of Kyle. I had been traumatized by his behavior, buried it the best I could, but it was destined to be resurrected. He engraved it into my subconscious. It was not my fault.

I contemplated for hours, which turned into days. I procrastinated because I was scared. As much as I wanted to do it, I couldn't. I didn't have the balls to do it.

I flushed the pills and burned my letters. Suicide was a selfish last resort.

I was restless, spending every day hidden away in my room with nothing to drink and little to do, so I turned to my guitar for some peace of mind. I was emotionally and physically wrecked and I was running out of options. Maybe guitar would help.

It did. It helped.

I vented through songwriting. It was an outlet for me to let out everything that had happened over the past few years. It was cathartic, and cleansing. You can't really appreciate the highs without the lows, and writing brought back some of the joy that had been absent from my life. The pain of that night with Victoria, and the pain of Jules's death, and Kyle… it all started to fade. I began to bury it, shoveling the dirt on top, one chunk at a time.

I realized I had gotten away with what I had done. My plan had worked. I had scared Victoria into silence. I'd outsmarted the laws of repercussion.

To make matters even better, my music flourished. My second album, *Hidden*, which I released that Fall, was one of the best I would ever create. It debuted online through iTunes mostly, and for whatever reason, the Gods deemed it worthy enough to sell a boatload of copies. After a few months, it peaked and broke into the *Billboard Hot 100 Albums* chart, which is kind of a big deal.

My hometown celebrity status increased tenfold.

*****

"What was your inspiration for this album?" The host of the local TV news channel, *Philly 101* asked me.

"It's about internal struggles with life and relationships," I said. "I found writing really helped me fight through the thick of what I was going through. I've grown a lot in the past few months…the past few years, really. It's cool to see how that changes your approach to your creative process."

"It seems to be helping a lot of others, too. *Hidden* has just peaked this week at #88 on the Billboard charts!"

I liked this host. She was cute. I wouldn't have minded an extended interview with her after the show. "It's incredible. I really can't believe it," I said.

"Your lyrics allude to a dark past…what happened exactly? If you don't mind my asking," she giggled, flipping a page in her notes.

"I keep it dark for a reason," I said.

"Not going to *shed a little light* on it for us?"

"Not today," I smiled back.

"Not even a snippet?"

I figured I'd give her a little, just so she'd leave me be. "A lot of it comes from one failed relationship in particular. I made a lot of mistakes, and I'd do things a lot differently if I had the chance to go back."

"Wow! Yes, I completely agree. I can think of so many instances in my life I would love to go back in time and change." She leaned back to talk to the audience. "We all do, don't we?" The crowd echoed a depressing "yes." "Any songs about time travel on your album, Tyler?"

"No," I said dryly. The camera op made a little twirling motion with his finger in the air like a tornado, signaling that our time was up. I could tell the host was a little bit heartbroken; her limelight gone until tomorrow.

I've always hated interviews.

* * * * *

Of course with my burgeoning acclaim and the increasing popularity of *Hidden*, all of my old friends, acquaintances, family, and people I hardly knew started calling. That's how success tends to work; no one wants to work for it or help you during the struggle, but once you've made it, they all want to be you. Everybody wants to be famous; no one wants to work for it!

"You're so lucky!"

No, I'm really not. Luck had no part in any of this. I worked for everything I've got.

I decided I couldn't go back to Penn State. I had changed too much, seen too much, done too much. I needed to restart. I needed somewhere new. I wanted to erase my history, and make friends with the type of people I truly get along well with, not just fake it. I'd managed to convert my anger into motivation. I had something to prove again. Everyone in Philly was lazy and ambition-less, like a pack of fat dogs lying in the shade waiting to be fed.

I was a lone wolf. It was time for me to venture onward and start a new wolf pack I could call my own.

CHAPTER TWENTY-SIX

I tossed the empty Bollinger bottle into the trash and raised my glass for a toast. "*Cheers.*"

Rachel was not amused. Her face was wet with tears, thick streams of black eyeliner flowing down her cheeks.

The sun was beating through the windows. It was gearing up to be a hot June afternoon. I found myself a glass of ice water and slurped it down loudly. I didn't feel the need to offer her one.

"Would you please let my security guards take you to the hospital?" I asked again. Her blood had seeped through the robe I had given her and was now leaving its mark on the white couch leather.

"Now, I know where the expression 'tortured artist' comes from," she said.

"That's not funny."

"Didn't mean for it to be." She took a moment, staring at her wiggling toes. "Seems like you won out in the end."

"I've done my fair share of losing," I said.

"The incredible *Tyler Clark!* The man who snuck out when no one was looking."

"I'm not running now."

"That's because I've got you trapped."

"I'm getting tired of this little back and forth. It's been a pleasure, but I've given you what you've asked for. I've told you what you wanted to hear."

She pulled out a small, folded up piece of paper from her bag. "I have something for you."

"What now—"

"It's from an old friend." She held it out to me. "Read it."

I took it and opened it. The handwriting was sloppy and scribbled, but I immediately recognized it. It was Kyle's handwriting. The letter was addressed to me.

Tyler,

I can only imagine how angry the thought of me probably makes you. I'm sorry, in so many ways, for the terrible things I did. The last time I saw you we were both in a courtroom we should have never seen the inside of. I wish I could take it back... I wish I could change it with all of my heart.

My father was mentally ill. Do you remember those nights on my front porch, when he would stumble home drunk, interrupting our guitar playing? I loved those jam sessions we had... night after night...all summer. Well...after you'd go home, my dad would grab me by the neck of my shirt and drag me into his room to abuse me. I thanked God every night he chose me instead of my sister. She was so sweet and innocent. I never bothered to show her how much I loved her. I did the opposite.

My life has been filled with regrets, Tyler, but none worse than what I did to you. I betrayed my closest friend in one of the worst ways imaginable. At the time I was high;

pills, cocaine, pot, the works. I'm not writing this to excuse my behavior; I'm writing to tell you the truth, because I won't get another chance to. I forced myself onto Jules like an animal and had my way with her like my father so often did to me.

I always loved Jules, you know that. There's that saying, "if you love someone enough you should be able to let them go." I should have let her go. Jules took her life because of me, and only *me. Don't ever think it had anything to do with you.*

I served time in juvie and jail, but no living sentence could ever pay back for the horrors I've committed.

I hope that one day, wherever you are, you can find it in your heart to forgive me. And if you can't... I understand. I hardly deserve it.

Kyle Hall

I folded up the note. I couldn't find words. My breaths were short, my throat was tight. I'd already been addressed in one suicide note—Jules', and that was one too many. I didn't ask for this. I didn't ask for any of this. *Why the fuck couldn't my fucking past stay buried?*

"He's at Jefferson Hospital right now, on life support. They say he only has a few days left," Rachel said. I pictured him, lying in a hospital bed on life support after attempting suicide, wishing he'd gotten it right the first time. What a fucking coward.

"What do you want me to do about it," I said.

"I want you to see him," she said.

"That's why you did this? All of this... beating yourself up, staging a rape, and forcing me to re-tell my entire life's story—"

"I'm sorry. I needed to hear your side of it."

"You could have just fucking asked!"

She rolled her eyes. "Because you would have told me…"

"How do you know Kyle?"

"I'll tell you at the hospital," she said. She stood up and started collecting her things.

"Did he tell you to do all of this?"

"I'll explain everything at the hospital."

"I'm not going to the hospital," I said. *Fuck you, Kyle Hall, you fucking arrogant son of a bitch. Always plotting, up until the minute you die.*

She held up that stupid fucking tape recorder again. "Are you his girlfriend?" I asked. She said nothing. If she was baiting me, I was falling for it. "Wow… I imagine he'll be thrilled when he finds out about last night."

Again, she gave me nothing. She bent over, picking up a few pens that had fallen off the table, purposely letting her towel slip down again.

"Why do you want me to see him?" I asked.

"Because I know he would really like it."

"How do you know that?"

"I just do. Now call your driver."

CHAPTER TWENTY-SEVEN

The hospital hallways bustled with doctors and nurses, running from room to room with charts in their hands, medical supplies, and trays of syringes. The sterility was uncomfortable.

"Hall. Room 413." Rachel said to the nurse at the desk. She had cleaned up well; none of the bruises and cuts were visible.

"Sign in, please," the nurse said without so much as glancing at us.

The walk down the hallway to his room felt like an eternity. I didn't want to see Kyle. I *never* wanted to see Kyle, and had made that the reality since the night he attacked Jules. Yet here I was, thanks to Rachel Helms of the goddamn *Philadelphia Inquirer*. She probably didn't even have a job. This whole thing was one big lie with Kyle behind the curtain, licking his lips and rubbing his hands together like the evil villain he is.

I couldn't ignore whatever it was inside of me, pulling at my soul, revving up a strange excitement. Oddly enough, part of me *wanted* to finally come face to face with Kyle. I wanted to punch him in his jaw until my hand broke; all of that old rage and hatred was bubbling up again. I could feel Jules' body, her touch, the taste of her lips. I could hear her laugh…see her smile. Suddenly I was launched back in time, to that last summer with her. Trudging through cornfields, watching the sun set over the tall grass. Laying on the hilltop with her next to me, staring up at the sky, enjoying the quiet…and then Kyle, slithering around in the shadows, with his weed, his pills, and his res-ridden bowls, eyelids heavy and bloodshot; planning to fuck her whether she liked it or not. I wondered when he had made the decision. Was it that night when Jules snuck down to me on the couch, and he woke up and saw us? I could still see the outline of his face, and the light reflecting from his dead black eyes, like it happened yesterday.

"Ouch!" Rachel said. I'd accidentally run into the back of her. I wasn't paying attention.

Room 413. There were baskets of flowers everywhere. American flags lined the walls, and Marine Corps hats, pins, t-shirts, and jackets were scattered among the tables and chairs. Rachel walked in and yanked the pale blue curtain back.

There he was. His face was a mess of black and blue bruises, and his body was covered in bandages. He was hardly recognizable. It looked like a freight train had run him over. Both arms were in casts, his head was supported by a neck brace, and his legs… they were gone.

He was staring at the muted TV in the corner. A rerun of "South Park."

"Kyle," Rachel whispered. He flinched a little, slightly surprised, and turned towards us.

I wanted to run. I wanted to be anywhere but here. He turned his head slowly, wincing in pain. He was about to speak, until he saw me.

I fought back tears with every ounce of strength. I'd wanted to knock him out, strangle him until he stopped breathing. I had dreamt of it so many nights after the trial. On the drive over I'd wanted to watch him die; unplug all of the wires and tubes shooting out of him and videotape him suffering in his final moments so I could watch it over and over, forever. But as soon as he looked at me, I couldn't. I was helpless. I wanted so badly to hug my old friend and never let go.

"Tyler," he said, in a raspy whisper. I cleared my throat. I grabbed on to the metal bedpost for support just in case.

We stood silently for a couple of minutes. Rachel was sitting in the chair beside him, holding his hand.

"What happened?" I finally managed to choke out.

"What, this?" he motioned to his non-existent legs, smiling. "IED got me on patrol in Mecca two days ago."

Rachel's tears were streaming.

"You're a Marine…" I said. "That wasn't a suicide note, was it."

Kyle chuckled, and then nearly coughed up a lung. He signaled Rachel for the bucket, which she put to his mouth as he spit up blood.

"I only have a few days left. I wanted you to know," he said.

"So you had your girlfriend stage a rape and blackmail me into coming here?"

Instantly, I knew he hadn't planned the set-up. He looked as shocked as I was. He turned to Rachel, who shrugged.

"I improvised," she said, trying to smile through her tears. "He wouldn't have listened."

She was right.

"Your girlfriend is fucking insane," I said.

"I didn't ask you here to argue," Kyle said. His body started convulsing violently. More vomiting. It was painful to watch him suffer. In my daydreams I enjoyed it, they got me through my anger and depression, but they were only dreams. This was real.

I was frustrated. I felt my fists and my jaw clenching. I didn't sign up for this.

"You're right. You didn't *ask* me here at all. Your loyal girlfriend here fucked me, and then *fucked* me, and now here we are."

He spit more blood into the bucket. "From what I've heard, it sounds like you and Emma got along rather well last night."

Emma? Who is Emma? "You mean Rachel, your psychopathic sidekick here?"

"No…" Kyle said.

"Emma." she said, quietly.

It hit me…It knocked the wind right out of me. It was like a swift kick to the throat. I couldn't believe it. I needed the bucket. I was going to throw up. This woman was not Rachel Helms of the *Inquirer*…she was Emma Hall, *Kyle's little sister*.

I dove into the bathroom and threw up in the toilet. I couldn't hold it in. The same poor chubby girl whom Kyle had kicked thirteen feet out of a tree house, I had in my bed. *How did I not recognize her?* From the minute she walked up I should have seen it! I'll admit I was a little drunk, but...*this whole time, the possibility never even dawned on me?*

I had figured Emma was long gone. Ditched her screwed-up family the minute she turned eighteen and moved across the country. That's what I'd hoped, for her sake.

But there she was.

I walked back to Kyle's bedside with what little dignity I still had. I was so shocked I couldn't speak.

"It's good to see you, Ty." Kyle said. "I've missed you."

Why did this hurt so horribly? This was Kyle, the guy who *raped* the love of my life.

Something about him had changed. I could see it in his eyes. The blackness had left.

"You're a good man... a much better man than me." He drifted off, gazing out the window.

I felt the tears welling up in my eyes. As I blinked they fell slowly down my cheeks, dropping peacefully to the floor. I had spent half of my life with this man. He was my brother.

"Three years ago, in October, my father came home from the bar, drunk as usual" he said. "We were living in Upper Darby then; a small house in a shitty neighborhood. I was up the street picking up a gallon of milk for breakfast the next day; I always hated going to the store in the morning.

"He stumbled in, and the only one home was my sister..." I watched him swallow hard, fighting to continue. "He hadn't come at me in years. I was too big, and could easily overpower him. I'd thought his sick spree had ended for good, but I was wrong. I came home to Emma's screams upstairs; he had locked the two of them in his bedroom. I broke down the door and ripped him off of her, knocking him around a bit. This was the first time he had ever come at her, so I was more upset than I'd ever been."

Tears plunged from his cheeks onto the bleached bed sheets. Emma gripped his hand tightly.

"I threw him down the first flight of stairs. Then the second... then down into the basement. I made sure he was conscious the whole time. He wasn't going to forget any of it." Emma let out a soft yelp, and dropped her head into her lap. Kyle wheezed for a minute, trying to catch his breath, trying not to spit up blood again. I didn't know what to do. I couldn't look Kyle in the eyes, so I closed mine and listened.

"I strung him up; tied his hands to the hot water pipes that run along the ceiling. I let him hang there for a few minutes." Kyle looked away from me, back out the window. "He'd ruined my life. The first time I was only twelve years old. *Twelve.* What kind of man does that? What kind of father..."

In retrospect, I don't know how I had missed the signs. The bruises on his neck, all those days when he would come over and not want to move, just sleep all day. His father *destroyed* him.

"I was always jealous of you, Ty." Kyle said.

I couldn't help but cut in a sad chuckle. "You? Jealous of *me?*"

"Your grandparents loved you so much. You had a real family."

I thought about my grandparents. I hadn't spoken to them in almost two months. I hadn't seen them in almost a year. I wanted to hug them, kiss them, laugh with them at the dinner table, and fall asleep with them by the fire reading our books. I wanted to love them the way they loved me. Kyle never got to experience that.

"I took my service pistol and I shot him. Three times in the chest, right through his heart." He turned and looked me dead in the eyes. "Then I burned the house down, with him in it."

Holy shit. I gripped the metal bedpost. *Holy shit.*

Kyle let out a groggy laugh. "You should see your face right now."

A tiny nurse with a ponytail and a heavy southern accent skipped into the room. "Hey, ya'll! How're ya'll doing? I see you've got some visitors Kyle, *this is so nice!*" She introduced herself as Carleen, and asked if we needed anything as she cleaned some of the blood from Kyle's mouth. We kindly declined. "Ok then, I'mma leave ya'll be, give ya'll some privacy! Kyle, just buzz me if you need anythang hunny buns."

She leaned in and whispered excitedly to Emma, "Don't forget his medicine, every half hour now cutie pie!"

Emma forced a smile as Carleen skipped back out of the room. You could hear her introduction to the patients next door through the walls.

I saw Kyle press and hold down the morphine button. His eyelids drooped.

"I know about Victoria," Kyle said. I shot a glance at Emma, who shrugged her shoulders. She must have already told him the whole thing. There was no sense in trying to play it off, so I opted for stoicism. "I met her at a support group a few years back, before I joined the Corps. She went to Penn State with you," he continued.

I was trying desperately to hide my trembling.

"We were the only two people our age in the support group, so we became friendly after a few meetings. She's such a sweet girl, and she helped me immensely; she's the reason I joined the Corps. Until that IED blew me in half, joining the Marines was the best decision I had ever made." I saw him click the morphine button again.

I pulled a chair over and sat down. I knew what was coming, and I didn't know if I could have stayed standing much longer.

"We confided in each other. We really connected; it felt safe to talk to her. I told her about my father, and she told me about you. What you did to her…how you threatened to kill her if she ever spoke out."

I looked down at the floor.

"We're not so different, after all," he said.

I was losing it. I could taste the warm salt of my tears.

"I don't even remember what happened, I just…reacted." I said.

"She was going to go to the police. I talked her out of it. That's not what she needed. She had so many great things going for her; the reputation of being a rape victim would have ruined it. I couldn't let her sabotage her future. And I couldn't let her do that to you."

Emma checked her watch, then tacitly opened a pill bottle

from the nightstand and poured two into her hand. She stood to fetch a water cup from the bathroom, but Kyle interrupted her.

"Not right now," he whispered.

"It's time for--"

"I said, *not now*. Please."

Frowning, she sat back down and placed the bottle back on the table.

"I need to ask one last favor of you," he said to me. I wiped my eyes with my sleeve and stood back up. "I need you to find Victoria, and apologize for what you've done."

"Kyle… I can't—"

"You don't want to live your life in guilt and regret, trust me. I never had the chance to tell Jules how sorry I was. You do."

"How can I just walk up to her—"

"Promise me you'll do it," he said.

My heart was racing. My legs were trembling under my weight. I didn't want to hear this. What Kyle was asking was impossible.

"Promise me…" He held out his hand. His eyeballs were drifting towards the back of his head, and his breathing had slowed almost to a complete stop. I grabbed his hand and gripped tight, trying to pull him back to consciousness.

"I promise," I said.

He smiled faintly, and then slid down in the bed, his head tilting backwards. I felt his grip loosening, and then watched his eyelids slowly close. I looked to his right hand; his thumb was white with pressure, hugging the morphine release button.

His thumb slowly changed from white to red. The grip of his palm in my hand lost its strength. The heart-rate monitor flat lined.

Kyle Hall was gone.

CHAPTER TWENTY-EIGHT

The funeral was gracious and somber, in traditional USMC fashion. Three shots were fired and Taps was played, and the flag was folded and presented to Emma. It hurt to see her so stricken with grief. She didn't deserve it. She'd been dealt an awful life, and still managed to overcome the adversity. Her eulogy was tasteful and eloquent, remembering a big brother for all of the good he brought to the world and those around him.

Watching Kyle's casket fade into the dirt was one of the most difficult moments of my life. I was saying goodbye for the second time…this time, forever. Films from our childhood played in my mind throughout the procession. Through my tears I found myself laughing, remembering the small things like his stupid evil villain cackle and his terribly screechy singing voice. I cried reminiscing his brilliant adventure ideas, his profound confidence, and his determination. He made decisions, and he pushed the pedal to the floor. Audacious and reckless, sure, but is confidence not a luxury reserved for the naive?

I would never forget twelve-year-old Kyle, my idol who became my best friend. My partner in crime. My brother.

The USMC took care of the funeral details and arrangements, which was a godsend. I helped Emma with the rest of the details like scheduling and invitations. Those first twenty-four hours that we were together were absolutely insane, but in a strange way, they brought us together. Shortly after Kyle passed, Emma destroyed the tape recording, admitted the bruises and cuts were fake, *and* that she didn't actually work at the *Inquirer* (I knew it). She had grabbed a job out of college in the makeup FX department of a film production company downtown and, after five too many low-budget slasher films, became a de-facto expert in cut and bruise FX and makeup, which is how she had faked the welts and lashings. It was an intense idea, but after looking at her resume, it made sense why she chose it. Kind of. Not really. By the end of our conversation, she'd confessed to me that she had faked everything but the sex. Kyle knew I would have never agreed to see him, or read his note, or allow any of what happened transpire, so he simply told Emma what she needed to know, and asked her to "improvise." She's always been creative.

I kept thinking about it. Re-playing that night over and over. Re-playing *her* over and over. Pretty soon the weirdness of Emma being Kyle's little sister disappeared. I actually started to kind of *like* her; she was fun, funny, and always cheerful.

"How you holding up?" I asked, slurping up the last few drops of my root beer. We'd made a pit stop at Chickie's & Pete's for a bite to eat after the funeral procession. Crab fries are always a good remedy for a down day.

"Welp, all the men in my family are dead," she said.

"In a couple more years I'll be right there with ya."

"Aww, don't say that! Your grandpa was always so nice to me; I love him."

"When was the last time you saw him?" I asked.

"Probably when I was eight or nine years old."

"Wow" I said, crunching down on the last of my fries. "He's changed a bit."

"All the more wiser, I'm sure."

"You could say that…"

"What would you say?" She asked.

"You should see for yourself…come with me to dinner tonight."

"I'm not going to barge in on your family dinner."

"Oh? You have other plans?"

"Why yes, I do. As a matter of fact I'm going… to go to the movies… and then have a glass of wine—"

"You mean a bottle—"

"A *bottle* of wine. Yes. Probably two," she smirked.

"You're coming to dinner with me," I said.

She grinned. I could tell the crab fries were working. "You'll love it. Granddad's grilling up his world-famous Teriyaki salmon steaks," I said. "No woman can resist his Teriyaki salmon steaks."

I paid the bill and we hit the road, heading back towards home. I was happy to see her smile, especially on a day like today. I clicked on the radio; Led Zeppelin's "The Ocean." *My fucking favorite!* I cranked the volume and rolled down the windows so that all could hear my glorious rendition.

"*Hitting on the moonshine! Rockin' in the gr—*"

The music abruptly cut off. Emma was staring at me.

"Just where exactly do you think you're taking us?" she asked.

"Uhh…home?"

"What about your apology?"

"…Apology?"

"Victoria." *Shit.* "Don't act like you don't know what I'm talking about, Tyler Clark." She loved calling me by my full name.

She knew I loved it.

"I haven't had time to look up her address," I said, reaching for the radio. She slapped my hand away and dug into her purse. She pulled out a small white slip of paper and handed it to me.

I reluctantly accepted. A scribbled address. Wonderful.

"I took the liberty of helping you out." She flashed a smile. I decided I didn't like her smile anymore.

"Ok…I'll go tomorr—"

"Right now."

I closed my eyes for a brief moment. This was a terrible, terrible idea. I stared ahead at the broken taillights of the bomber Cavalier chugging along in front of us, then over at Emma's scowling face, then back.

I flicked my turn signal on.

CHAPTER TWENTY-NINE

We pulled up about half a block short of Victoria's house. I refused to drive any closer.

"Well…" Emma said.

"Would you just hold on a second? Can we at least wait *two minutes* to see if she's even home?"

"Oh my god, chill out there, bro."

"You chill out," I said, like I was in fifth grade again, *still* with no good comebacks. I slunk into my seat.

"Are you sure you want to be here?" I asked her, genuinely. This seemed so close to home for her. Especially today.

"We've all made mistakes," she said.

"Not like this," I said, ashamed.

"You're right. But while that may be true, I like to believe God forgives. I like to think He forgave my father, and that He forgave Kyle, and that they are both in a good place."

I bowed my head, thinking about Kyle again. And Jules…I hoped she was in a better place than where I was probably headed.

"Most of all, you need to apologize so you can forgive yourself" she said.

I was running about a million and one hypothetical conversations over in my head. Would Victoria scream? Run? Attack me? Shoot me? Would she even recognize me? Her house was big. She definitely didn't live here alone. What if her husband, or brother, or father were in town? And what if they were all dishonorably discharged ex-military guys just *looking* for a punk like me to strangle? Fuck my life. Seriously.

I got out, slowly, reluctantly, my body preparing for instant cardiac arrest. I faced the house. Breathed in deep through my nose, then slowly out my mouth. This would never make up for what I'd done, but I still had to do it. Not only for Kyle, and for Emma, and for myself...but for Victoria.

The front door of the house swung open. A little four-year-old girl ran out, dressed in a tiny pink tutu. I was too far away to hear what was said, but she happily squealed something and was followed out by her father, who slung a pink gym bag over his shoulder, and her mother, holding an infant in her arms, trying to lock the door shut behind her. Victoria.

I recognized her instantly. It was the same face that I once saw cowering in the corner of a dorm room, shivering with fear. Today it was glowing with warmth and joy. Her husband ran back and helped her with the door. Together they battled to get the squirming little girl and the crying baby into their car seats, high-fived to their accomplishment, and went to hop into their minivan.

Then she saw me. She did a double-take and froze on the spot. She must have recognized me. No one would stop and stare like that if they didn't.

The moment was suspended for an eternity; neither of us could look away. In my predictions, I had expected her to turn ghastly white and scream, drop her things, dive into the minivan as it peeled off, fleeing from her rapist stalker like it were some action thriller movie. Instead, I was the one who went white. Victoria hardly flinched. She was calm. She was very aware of the situation; like a deer when a twig snaps—still chewing his grass—but with his head up and his ears perked. There was an electricity wisping between us, forever bonded by that night in college, never wanting to talk about it, but always hoping to find out the why's and how's of it all.

I was glad to see how happy she was with her family and her children. In that moment, nothing could have made me happier. What I had done to Victoria hadn't turned her into a damaged psychopath, or a junkie, or a pregnant teen-mom with a meth addiction. The relief was prodigious. She was a healthy wife and a loving mother now; and she had a husband who probably loved her to death. Maybe, ten or twenty years from now, she would tell him what happened, and together they would get through it. Hopefully, he wouldn't hunt me down and kill me; but even If he did, I would die willingly. I would deserve a death by his hand.

In those brief two or three seconds, I knew that things would be ok. I could never make up for what I had done, but I would try. Forever, I would try. I was eternally in her debt; her silence had allowed me to continue on, to chase down my career, to become the man I am today. And she was strong. Much stronger than me. She fought through the silence and found love. *Real* love.

I vowed I would repay her.

Then, as if it had never happened, the moment passed. Victoria turned, got into the minivan with the rest of her family, and was gone.

Dave Patten

Renaissance man may be the best way to describe musician, writer, producer and actor Dave Patten, whose creative passions often necessitate more time for work than sleep.

2013 has been a breakout year for Dave with the publishing of his first novel, "Run of The Mill," a dramatic story about a rich playboy who must come to terms with his demons, and the release of his film in November, Delivery Man, from DreamWorks, alongside Vince Vaughn.

Dave's trajectory and creative drive can all be connected to his love of music. Growing up around everything from classical to R&B, Dave quickly took to the drums, mastering his skill-set with local bands. However, Dave didn't stop there, conquering the piano, guitar, bass, trumpet, trombone and cello, which not only allowed him to hone his unique sound, but write and produce his own music as well. With a mix of acoustic, rock and synthesized melodies, his cross-genre style has garnered much attention. In 2006 Dave began posting videos on YouTube, amassing over 60 million page views and a social network following numbering in the thousands, and growing exponentially.

While Dave was perfecting his craft, he crossed paths with rap artist Meek Mill, another Philadelphia native. Meek and Dave quickly bonded leading this unlikely partnership into a unique collaboration and Dave signing to Meek's label, DreamChasers Records. Dave grew up in Philadelphia, entrenching himself in the music scene there. As he made a name for himself in local venues, Dave continually strived to learn and grow as an artist. Dave continuously searches out unique and interesting projects that allow him any and all opportunities for creative outlet.

We'd like to thank you for supporting G Street Chronicles and invite you to join our social networks. Please be sure to post a review when you're finished reading.

Like us on Facebook
G Street Chronicles
G Street Chronicles CEO Exclusive Readers Group

Follow us on Twitter
@GStreetChronicl

Follow us on Instagram
gstreetchronicles

Email us and we'll add you to our mailing list
fans@gstreetchronicles.com

George Sherman Hudson, CEO
Shawna A., COO